Cul-de-Sac K[...]

Collection Two

BOOKS BY BEVERLY LEWIS

Picture Books

Annika's Secret Wish
In Jesse's Shoes
Just Like Mama
What Is God Like?
What Is Heaven Like?

Children's Fiction

CUL-DE-SAC KIDS °

Cul-de-Sac Kids Collection One
Cul-de-Sac Kids Collection Two

Youth Fiction

GIRLS ONLY (GO!) *

Girls Only! Volume One
Girls Only! Volume Two

SUMMERHILL SECRETS +

SummerHill Secrets Volume One
SummerHill Secrets Volume Two

HOLLY'S HEART +

Holly's Heart Collection One
Holly's Heart Collection Two
Holly's Heart Collection Three

www.beverlylewis.com

* 4 books in each volume   + 5 books in each volume   ° 6 books in each volume

Cul-de-Sac Kids
Collection Two

BOOKS 7–12

Beverly Lewis

BETHANYHOUSE
a division of Baker Publishing Group
Minneapolis, Minnesota

© 1996, 1997 by Beverly Lewis

Previously published in six separate volumes:
   The Stinky Sneakers Mystery © 1996
   Pickle Pizza © 1996
   Mailbox Mania © 1996
   The Mudhole Mystery © 1997
   Fiddlesticks © 1997
   The Crabby Cat Caper © 1997

Published by Bethany House Publishers
11400 Hampshire Avenue South
Bloomington, Minnesota 55438
www.bethanyhouse.com

Bethany House Publishers is a division of
Baker Publishing Group, Grand Rapids, Michigan

Printed in the United States of America

ISBN 978-0-7642-3049-3

Library of Congress Control Number: 2017945876

Scripture in *Fiddlesticks* quoted from the International Children's Bible®,
copyright © 1986, 1988, 1999, 2015 by Tommy Nelson. Used by permission.

These stories are works of fiction. Names, characters, incidents, and dialogues
are products of the author's imagination and are not to be construed as real.
Any resemblance to any person, living or dead, is purely coincidental.

Cover design by Eric Walljasper
Cover illustration by Paul Turnbaugh
Story illustrations by Janet Huntington

17 18 19 20 21 22 23   7 6 5 4 3 2 1

Contents

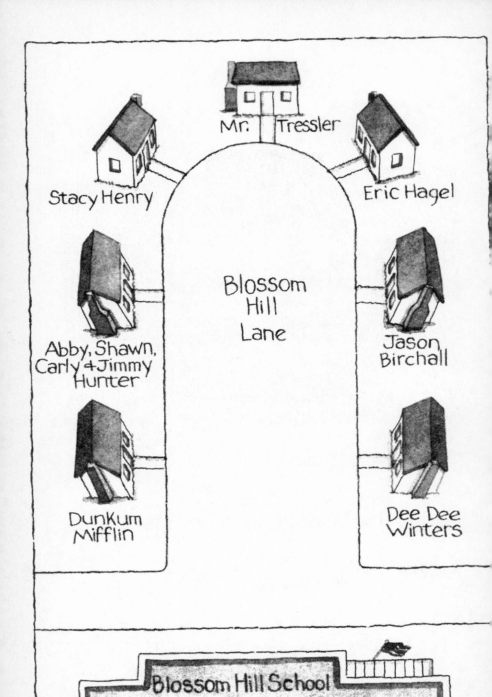

BOOK 7

The Stinky Sneakers Mystery

To
Darrel Barnes
(Surprise!)

One

Jason Birchall wanted first place in the science fair. So did *all* the kids in Miss Hershey's class.

But Jason was the only one bragging about his project.

He bragged to his friends Eric, Shawn, and Dunkum. He bragged during math, at lunch, and all during recess.

Jason was still talking about his project on the walk home from school. "I'm getting first place this year," he said. "Can you guess why?"

Eric Hagel and Shawn Hunter shook their heads. "Nope," said Eric.

"Nope," repeated Shawn. "I not." He was

still learning English. Shawn and his brother, Jimmy, had come from Korea.

"Hurry up, Jason. Spit it out," Dunkum Mifflin said. "What's so great about your project?"

Jason spotted Abby Hunter and her best friend, Stacy Henry. "Hey, girls," he called to them. "Want to hear about my science project?"

Abby and Stacy didn't even turn around. They whispered to each other instead.

They're really dying to know, thought Jason.

In the middle of the cul-de-sac, Jason stopped. He put his hands up to his mouth and shouted, "I have the best science project in the world!"

Abby glanced over her shoulder. "You're going to make yourself disappear, right?"

Stacy Henry giggled.

Eric and Shawn tried not to.

"Very funny," said Jason.

"Come on," Dunkum said. "Give it to us straight. What's your project?"

"Yes, give us *good* hint," Shawn said.

Jason folded his arms across his chest. He looked at his cul-de-sac friends.

"Super sprouts," he said, the words shooting past his lips. "I'm growing super sprouts."

Eric laughed. "Anyone can do that."

"Not the way *I'm* growing them," Jason said.

"What's so special about it?" asked Dunkum.

Jason's voice got louder. "My sprouts are growing in a piece of carpet."

Shawn looked puzzled. "Magic sprouts?"

Eric's eyes got wide. But he was silent.

Shawn grinned at Jason. "You get first place!"

"You're right!" Jason shouted. "And next week, we'll find out!"

"We sure will," Eric said. There was a sly grin on his face. A very sly grin.

Now Jason was worried. He watched Eric run up the steps to his house.

What was *Eric's* project? And why was he acting so strange?

TWO

Jason was counting. Three more days until the science fair.

He sat on the beanbag chair in his room. He was trying to do math. Ten problems for tomorrow.

Jason groaned. He was only half finished.

He couldn't keep his mind on math. He gazed at the windowsill. The super sprouts were growing there in a piece of green carpet.

Jason stared at them. He stared hard.

He imagined a giant trophy floating over the sprouts.

Jason could hear Miss Hershey's voice. She was telling the class about his project. Miss Hershey was bragging about him.

"Now, for the best student in the class," she said. "Will Jason Birchall please come forward?"

The other kids were green with envy.

Abby and Stacy were pointing.

Eric and Dunkum were leaning forward in their seats.

Everyone was whispering, *Jason . . . Jason . . .* His name flew around the classroom.

Jason stood up and went to Miss Hershey's desk. All eyes were on him.

The teacher held up a shiny gold trophy. First place!

"Wow," said the kids.

Jason held up his green carpet square and the super sprouts. He held them high.

"Jason! Yippee!" The whole class cheered. Wild, happy cheering.

■■■

Zzz. Jason was asleep in his beanbag.

The phone rang. Jason jumped.

His mother called to him, "It's your friend Eric."

Jason rubbed his eyes. He pulled himself out of the beanbag. "I'm coming," he mumbled.

He shuffled down the hallway. His mother held out the phone.

"Hello?" Jason said.

"Hi," Eric said. "You know that sprout project of yours?"

Jason yawned. "Uh-huh."

"Well, don't plan on winning first place." Eric sounded too sure of himself.

"Why not?" Jason asked.

"Because there's no chance," Eric replied. "No chance you'll get first place."

Jason took off his glasses. He stared at them. "That's what *you* think!" he said and hung up the phone.

■■■

The next day was Tuesday. Eric was absent from school. He never missed!

Jason felt jumpy. He got that way when he didn't take his pills. Being an A.D.D. kid was hard. But the pills helped him think about his work.

Today was different. He'd taken his pills at breakfast, but he was still jumpy. Jason jittered. He twittered.

Something kept zipping around in his

brain. He worried all through math and history. Through recess and lunch.

Eric Hagel was *never* sick. Why had he stayed home?

During afternoon recess, Dunkum shot baskets with Jason. "Stop worrying," Dunkum said. "Eric's probably just sick."

"How do you know?" Jason asked.

Dunkum shrugged. "I don't."

Jason told him about Eric's sneaky smile. Then he told him about Eric's phone call. "He's acting weird," Jason said.

Dunkum only laughed. "Eric wouldn't stay home to do a science project. No way!"

Jason dribbled the ball. He aimed, shot, and missed. "Well, I think something's up."

Dunkum's turn. He shot and made it. "You'll see. There's probably nothing to worry about."

The bell rang.

Jason raced into the school building. *Maybe Dunkum is right,* he thought. *Maybe there isn't anything to worry about.*

He went to his desk and opened his math book. But Jason couldn't get Eric's sly smile out of his mind.

"Jason," Miss Hershey called, "please come to the board."

Jason went. He tried not to look at Eric's empty desk.

Why had Eric stayed home?

What was *really* going on?

Three

The last bell rang.

Jason didn't walk home with the Cul-de-Sac Kids. He ran straight to Eric's house. Right up to his front porch.

Eric's grandpa was sitting in a wicker chair. "Hello, Jason," Mr. Hagel said.

"How are you today?" Jason asked.

The old man chuckled. "Not too bad for my age."

Jason wondered, *Should I ask about Eric?*

Mr. Hagel peered over his newspaper. "If you're looking for Eric, he's upstairs in bed."

Jason remembered what Dunkum had said. "Is . . . is Eric too sick for company?" he asked.

"My goodness, no." Mr. Hagel waved his

hand. "Go wake him. He's sleeping the daylight away."

Jason wondered about that. "What's wrong with Eric?"

"Ah, nothing a good night's sleep won't cure."

"Sleep?" Jason said. "Eric's not sick?"

The old man shook his head. "My grandson is mighty busy these days. I think he was up half the night."

"Busy with science?" Jason asked.

Mr. Hagel chuckled. "That's right."

Jason opened the screen door and marched into Eric's house. Up the stairs and right into his friend's bedroom.

Eric was working at his desk. Still wearing pj's.

"Looks like you're not very sick," Jason said.

Eric leaped out of his chair. He stood in front of his desk. "What . . . what are you doing here?"

Jason inched closer, but Eric didn't move.

"I asked what you're doing here."

Jason pushed up his glasses. "Your grandpa told me to wake you."

Eric shook his head. "I don't believe you."

"Go and ask," Jason said.

"It's a trick," Eric said. "You just want to see my science project."

"You're wrong, Eric." Jason turned to go.

"You think you're so smart," Eric continued. "But, Jason Birchall, you just wait!"

Jason wanted to bop his friend. He really wanted to. But he made a fist inside his pocket and punched it into his pants. Then he headed for the steps.

"No, *you* wait," Jason muttered.

Four

It was Wednesday.

One more day till the science fair began.

Miss Hershey's class was ready. Especially Jason.

At recess, he started bragging again. "*My* project will take first place."

Eric sat on a swing. He pushed his foot into the sand. He was never like this. Too quiet.

Jason wondered why.

Dunkum and Shawn came over. "What's up?" Dunkum asked.

Jason said, "Eric's not talking."

Dunkum laughed. "Why not?"

Shawn spoke up. "Maybe still sick?"

Jason shouted, "He was never sick!"

Jason paced back and forth in the sand. He wondered why Eric was keeping his project a secret. It worried him.

Abby and Stacy came over. They wanted to swing.

Eric got off and went to play ball. Dunkum and Shawn left, too.

Jason started to leave. Then he heard Abby tell Stacy about her project.

"I can make it rain," Abby said.

Stacy giggled. "Sounds drippy."

Jason hung around. Abby's project sounded terrific.

Abby laughed with her best friend. "It's simple. All you need is an ice-cold soup dipper and a teapot."

Jason couldn't believe his ears. Where did Abby get such a good idea?

Then Stacy told Abby about *her* project. Jason crept closer.

"My project is called 'A Tight Squeeze,'" said Stacy. "I'm going to show how to make a giant hole out of paper."

"Sounds easy." Abby began to swing.

"Big enough to put over your head? Oh,

and the paper can't rip while you do it," Stacy explained.

Abby stopped swinging. "Now, *that* sounds hard."

"Sure does," Jason said.

The girls looked up. "You were snooping!" Abby said.

Jason grinned.

"By the way, how are your super sprouts doing?" Abby asked.

Jason stood tall. He stuck out his chest. "My sprouts are super, and they're sprouting. That's how they're doing."

The girls giggled. "What a silly project," Stacy said.

"Is not!" Jason replied.

They began to chant. "Jason's growing super sprouts . . . super sprouts . . . super sprouts."

Then they started giggling again.

Jason couldn't stand it. He ran to the ball field.

The girls had no right to make fun of his sprouts.

Super or not.

Five

On the way home from school, Dunkum told about his science project. "I'm doing a taste test."

"You're going to feed us?" Jason said.

Dunkum nodded. "Just some turnips, carrots, and apple."

"Sounds yucky," Jason said.

"Bet you can't tell the difference between them," Dunkum said.

"Bet I can," Jason said. "Easy!"

Dunkum's eyebrows shot up. "We'll see."

Shawn nodded. "Dunkum have super tongue."

Dunkum chuckled.

But Eric was silent.

"What about *your* project?" Jason asked Shawn.

"I make you see sound," he said. "I make sound dance on wall."

"Are you joking?" Jason asked. "You can't do that!"

Shawn's dark eyes were shining. "You will see."

"Tomorrow," Dunkum said.

"Tomorrow!" Jason shouted. But he was thinking about *his* project. Not Shawn's.

Jason dashed home to check his sprouts.

His mother was waiting at the door. "Time for a snack." She gave him a hug.

Jason took his afternoon pill with his snack. Then he ran to his room.

Sunshine poured onto the windowsill.

He hurried over to his super sprouts. Bright green.

Next, he touched the long carpet square. Damp.

Jason grinned. He found his notebook and wrote down the supplies and steps.

1. Shallow box
2. Plastic trash bag lining

3. Scrap of carpet

4. Alfalfa seeds

5. Some sunshine

6. Water

7. And . . . super sprouts!

He signed his name to the science paper. Everything was ready.

Jason went outside to ride his bike.

Eric was across the street at Dunkum's house. He was carrying a folder. A large black one.

When Jason got back from his ride, Eric was coming out of Abby and Shawn's house. What was he doing?

Jason zipped down the street, pretending not to care. He rode to the school playground and hid behind a tree. He spied as Eric headed to Stacy's house.

Eric rang the doorbell, and Stacy let him in.

This is weird, thought Jason. *Eric is up to something. Something very strange!*

Six

Snooping on Eric is great! thought Jason. He watched Eric go to Mr. Tressler's house next. Mr. Tressler and Eric's grandpa were good friends.

Eric rang the doorbell and waited. Mr. Tressler let him in.

Jason waited, still hiding behind the tree.

Soon, Eric came out. He headed to Jason's house.

Quickly, Jason hopped on his bike. He had to know what Eric was doing!

Jason flew down Blossom Hill Lane. He braked in front of his house.

Eric stopped on Jason's driveway and frowned.

"What's up?" Jason asked.

"Can I borrow your thumb?" Eric asked.

"My thumb?" Jason said. "What for?"

Eric smiled. "For my science project."

Jason got off his bike. He folded his arms across his chest. "I'm not helping *you*. And that's final."

"But—"

"You heard me!" Jason shouted. And he stomped into the house.

■ ■ ■

Thirty minutes later, Jason's doorbell rang. He was ready to sock Eric in the nose.

Jason grabbed the doorknob.

It was Stacy Henry. She was holding her white cockapoo puppy. His name was Sunday Funnies—because he always found the Sunday comics first. Before anyone!

Stacy's science folder was tucked under her arm. "I need to test my project," she said. "Can you help me?"

Jason didn't want to at first. Why was everyone asking for his help?

"Please?" Stacy said. "It won't take long."

He opened the screen door. "Okay."

They went into the kitchen. Stacy put her

puppy down on the floor. She took out a piece of paper and some scissors from her folder.

"Here," she said. "Try to cut a hole big enough to pass over your body."

Jason picked up the scissors. "Easy."

While he cut, Stacy asked about his project. "Can I see your super sprouts?"

"Only if you don't laugh at them," he said. He put the paper and scissors on the table.

"I promise."

"Okay then," Jason said.

He went to his room and came right back, carrying the box. Inside, the carpet was full of bushy green sprouts.

She sniffed the sprouts. "Smells good. May I taste?"

"Just a little," Jason said. "I need lots of them for tomorrow."

Stacy pulled off a tiny sprig and put it in her mouth. "Mm-m, good!"

Sunday Funnies stood up on his hind legs.

Stacy laughed. "Look, my dog wants a bite, too."

"I can't let a dog eat my first-prize project!"

"Aw, just a little?" Stacy pleaded.

The puppy was still begging.

Jason refused to look at Stacy's dog. "How long is he going to do that?"

"Till he gets what he wants," she said.

Jason frowned. He looked at Sunday Funnies. "Oh, all right. Give him a taste."

Sunday Funnies ate the sprouts, then licked his chops.

"He loves them!" Stacy exclaimed.

"I was afraid of that," Jason said. He picked up the paper and scissors and began to cut again.

Stacy watched him. "Can you do it? Can you make a hole fit over your head?" she asked.

He slid the circle halfway over his head. It was too small to go farther.

Stacy said, "I think you're stuck."

Jason pulled the paper off his head. "This is impossible."

"Here, I'll show you how," Stacy said.

Sunday Funnies was begging again, Jason noticed. "Put my sprouts away," he said. He pointed to the top of the refrigerator.

Stacy stood on a chair and put the box up there. Now the sprouts were safe.

When Stacy got down, she took another

piece of paper and folded it in half—long, like a hot dog. She made thirteen cuts on the folded paper.

Jason watched carefully.

Gently, she stretched the paper out. And climbed through.

"Wow, that's cool!" Jason said. But he didn't really mean it. Stacy's project was too good.

Stacy picked up her folder, scissors, and paper. She walked to the front door. Sunday Funnies followed.

"Thanks for your help," she said.

Jason closed the door without saying a word.

Seven

Jason yawned. He opened his eyes.

Thursday at last!

He flew down the hall to the bathroom and washed his face. He got dressed in record time.

At breakfast, Jason took his pill without a fuss. And he ate everything on his plate.

"This is a very big day," his father said.

"Sure is," his mother said.

"My sprouts are super!" Jason said. "They're the very best!"

His parents smiled at him across the table.

Jason looked at his watch. "It's too early for school."

"You could start gathering up your things," his mother suggested.

His father patted him on the back. "Have a great science fair," he said and left for work.

His mother went to take her shower.

Jason scampered to his room and found his notebook. He'd been counting the hours. The fair started today. It would end tomorrow with the judging.

He couldn't wait.

Then Jason remembered Stacy's paper hole project, and Abby's homemade rain.

Shawn was going to make sound dance on the wall. Dunkum had a turnip taste test.

But what about Eric? What was *he* doing?

Quickly, Jason went to the windowsill. Time to take his super sprouts to school. But . . .

The sprouts were gone!

"Where's my project?"

He searched his room. Then he ran through the house. But his sprouts were nowhere to be seen.

Gone!

"Where are they?" he wailed.

He called to his mother through the bathroom door.

She didn't answer.

Jason pounded on the door. "Mom!"

"I'm in the shower," she called back. "I can't hear you."

Jason stood in the middle of the living room. He shook with worry. *What can I do?*

A huge lump crowded his throat.

Then he heard sounds outside. Running to the window, he looked out.

The Cul-de-Sac Kids were walking to school together. They bunched up in front of his house. Waiting.

Jason opened the front door. "Wait a minute," he called.

He couldn't tell them about his missing sprouts. After all his bragging, he just couldn't!

Jason ran around the house searching for something. Anything. What could he use for a science project?

He looked under his bed and found some dirty socks. Yuck! He held his nose.

He thought of Shawn's project—making sound dance on the wall. Maybe he could make smells dance, too.

No. That was silly.

He ran to the window. The kids were still waiting—with their science projects.

"Hurry up!" Abby called from the street.

Jason banged into the kitchen. He looked around for something to take for the science fair. But there was nothing. Nothing!

So much for first place, he thought.

Miss Hershey would give him a big fat zero!

Eight

Jason heard a knock on the screen door.
"Come in," he said.

In came the Cul-de-Sac Kids.

Abby and Stacy.

Dunkum, Shawn, and Shawn's little brother, Jimmy. Abby's little sister, Carly, with her best friend, Dee Dee Winters.

And Eric.

"Where's your science project?" Abby asked.

Jason was speechless.

"Yeah, let's see those super sprouts," Eric said.

"I . . . uh . . ." Jason knew they would laugh. He couldn't tell them.

Stacy looked at her watch. "We better get going. We don't want to be late."

The kids were too excited to wait for Jason. They left for school. Without him.

Jason decided to look outside for his sprouts. He went around the side of the house.

He sniffed the air. He coughed. Something smelled rotten, like three-week-old gym socks!

Eric's grandpa was sitting on the porch next door. "Good morning, Jason," he said.

Jason stepped closer. "What's that smell?"

Mr. Hagel was spreading cheese on some bread. "This, young man, is my favorite cheese. It's called Limburger."

Jason pinched his nose shut. "Smells horrible!"

Mr. Hagel grinned. "Ah, but the taste is out of this world. Care for some?"

"I . . . uh . . . better not." Jason stepped back, away from the odor.

"Just try it," Mr. Hagel said. "Have it in your lunch, maybe." He wrapped a lump of it in plastic and gave it to Jason.

"Uh . . . thanks." Jason stuffed the nasty-smelling cheese into his pocket. He would toss it in the trash later.

■■■

At school, the kids were lining up outside. Their hands were filled with science projects.

Jason got in line. He hid his hands in his pants pockets.

Eric teased, "Hey, Sprout Man, tell the truth. You didn't really make a project, did you?"

Jason felt his neck get hot. "You're wrong!" He ran up to Eric.

Stacy and Abby pushed the boys apart. "Stop it!" Stacy yelled. "I saw Jason's sprouts yesterday."

Eric looked surprised. "Oh, really? Well, where are they now?"

"Disappeared," Jason muttered. "They're missing."

Shawn frowned. "Missing from earth?"

"No, from Jason's house," Abby explained.

"Too bad," Shawn said. "I want to see super sprouts."

Eric snickered. "You're not the only one!"

Jason stuffed his hands into his pockets again. His fingers bumped the mound of smelly cheese. Eric's grandpa's cheese.

And suddenly, he had a great idea.

Nine

The mats were out in PE. It was tumbling day.

Jason and the rest of the class lined their shoes up along the wall.

Then they warmed up with three forward rolls each. Next came three backward rolls. Some kids did handstands.

Jason took off his glasses and did two backflips with help. Dunkum did a handstand for five seconds.

Eric stood on his head without wobbling. Shawn practiced walking on his hands.

Abby and Stacy did double cartwheels.

Whew! Jason's mouth was getting dry. He needed a long, cold drink.

So did Eric. And Dunkum.

The teacher let Jason go first. Then Eric. They were only allowed to go one at a time.

Eric came back from the water fountain. "Mr. Sprout Man gets a zero," he teased.

"Leave me alone," Jason shot back.

Eric scrunched up his face. "How could you lose a science project? That's dumb."

Jason was boiling mad. He needed another drink. The teacher said he could have one more.

Hurrying toward the drinking fountain, Jason passed the row of sneakers. He spotted Abby's red and blue ones.

He saw Shawn's blue sneakers.

Here's my chance, he thought. And he dug into his pocket and pulled out the smelly cheese.

After class, the teacher blew her whistle twice. Time to get shoes back on.

Quickly, Jason found his sneakers.

He heard Abby squeal, "This is so yucky!"

"Gross!" Eric said.

"Pee-yew!" Stacy shouted.

Jason jumped up. "What's that smell?" He pinched his nose shut.

"Very big stink," Shawn said. He pushed

his foot into his sneaker. His eyes bugged out. "Something feel mushy inside." Shawn yanked his foot out.

Abby came over to see. "Yuck!" she said. "You've got rotten cheese in there, too."

"So do I," Eric hollered.

"Me too," called Stacy.

"Me three," said Abby. "Who *did* this?"

Eric shook his sneakers out. "Smells like Grandpa's cheese!"

Abby's eyebrows flew up. "Why'd you put your grandpa's cheese in our sneakers?"

"I'd never do that!" Eric held up his own pair of sneakers, shaking his head.

By now, Miss Hershey was waiting in the hall. "Time to line up," she called.

"I'm not wearing these sneakers anymore," Abby told Eric.

Stacy, Shawn, and Eric agreed. They went to class in their socks.

Jason followed, holding his nose.

Abby got in line. "My sneakers are ruined," she said. "I can't believe Eric did this!"

Eric pushed ahead in line. "I told you, I *didn't* do it!"

46

"Right," Abby said. "And I don't believe you."

Jason didn't smile. He didn't laugh. But he wanted to—right in Eric's face.

Serves him right, he thought.

Ten

In the classroom, Jason hurried to his desk.

Miss Hershey held a hankie over her nose. "This room smells terrible," she said. "Who knows about this?"

Shawn said, "My *nose* does!"

The kids laughed. So did Miss Hershey. "My nose knows, too," she said.

In came the janitor with three big fans.

Jason and Dunkum opened all the windows.

Abby and Stacy made paper fans.

Then science class got started.

Miss Hershey called Dunkum's name. He did his taste test, but nobody could taste a thing. They all were holding their noses shut.

Dunkum explained, "This experiment proves my point. You can't taste unless you can smell."

Abby and Stacy started coughing. Jason pretended to gag.

Dunkum's eyes watered. "Make it rain, Abby," he said. "Quick!"

"Yes," Miss Hershey said. "A good rain might clear the air."

Abby did her homemade rain project, with her teapot of hot water and soup dipper. But afterward, the smell was still strong.

Next, Stacy had the whole class cutting holes. "My project is called 'A Tight Squeeze,'" she said. "I will show how paper can stretch."

It was hard holding noses and handling scissors and paper. So Stacy showed the class how the cutting was done.

Then it was Eric's turn.

Some of the kids hissed. Jason started to boo.

"Class," Miss Hershey said. "That's *not* polite."

"But Eric put Limburger cheese in our sneakers," Stacy said.

Miss Hershey looked at Eric and frowned.

"I didn't do it," he said. "And I can prove it!"

Jason sat tall in his seat. He was worried.

Eric set up his science project. "This is a fingerprint experiment," he explained. "I made a record of fingerprints." He pointed to a grouping of prints mounted on poster board.

He showed the class how to make finger-prints and how to dust for them.

"Now," he said. "I will prove that I didn't plant the Limburger cheese."

Jason leaned forward. He had to see this.

Eric held up a piece of cheese. "There's a thumbprint on this." He pinched his nose shut with his other hand. "You can't see it, but it's there."

Jason squirmed.

Eric continued. "The thumbprint on the cheese doesn't match mine," he said. "It doesn't match any of the prints I have."

Miss Hershey asked, "How many thumb-prints did you take?"

Eric looked around the room. "I recorded everyone in the class." He looked at Jason. "Everyone, except one."

Jason squirmed even more.

Eric grinned. "I think I solved the stinky sneakers mystery."

Abby raised her hand. "Whose thumbprint is missing?"

"Jason's," he said.

Jason stood up without being asked. He went to the front of the room.

All eyes were on him.

Eric opened his black ink pad. "Press your right thumb here," he said.

Jason pushed his thumb down. The pad felt gooey.

Eric pointed to a piece of paper. "Roll your thumb on this."

Jason obeyed. Then he lifted his thumb off the paper and looked down. Oval lines were where his thumb had been.

"Let's see if they match," Eric said. He compared Jason's thumbprint and the print on the cheese.

Miss Hershey watched closely.

All the kids stared.

Three fans hummed.

And Jason's heart thumped. Hard.

Eleven

Miss Hershey stood up.

Jason . . . Jason . . . His name flew around the room.

"Quiet, please," Miss Hershey said.

Jason wanted to hide.

"I want you to stay after school," his teacher said. "Do you understand why?"

Jason nodded. "Yes, Miss Hershey."

After school, Jason wrote fifty times: *I will treat others with respect.*

Then Jason took the paper to Miss Hershey. "I have something to tell you," he said.

Miss Hershey looked up.

"I'm sorry about the stinky sneakers." Jason took a deep breath. "I just—" He paused.

"What is it, Jason?"

"Eric just made me so mad. I couldn't find my project this morning, and Eric made fun. He said I didn't even have one. But I *did*. A really super—" He stopped.

He didn't want to brag about the sprouts. Bragging had gotten him in big trouble.

Jason's voice grew soft. "I lost my science project."

"Can you find it by tomorrow?"

Jason felt better. "I hope so."

Miss Hershey smiled. "So do I."

Jason couldn't believe his ears. Tomorrow was the judging. If he found his sprouts, they might still win first place!

He ran all the way home.

■■■

At home, Jason searched for his sprouts.

He looked in the garage and on the back deck. He looked under the front porch. He even searched the attic.

But his project was missing. Maybe forever!

Then the doorbell rang.

Jason's mother called to him.

He sat on the beanbag chair in his room feeling sad. "Who is it?"

"Your friends are here to see you."

Jason sighed. He didn't move an inch.

Soon, he heard giggling. It was Stacy and Abby. He'd know their giggles anywhere.

Jason got up and scurried down the hall. The living room was full of kids—the Cul-de-Sac Kids.

Stacy and Abby were still giggling. And now his mother was, too!

"What's so funny?" Jason asked.

Abby poked her hands in her pocket. "Oh, nothing."

Stacy tried to stop laughing.

Dunkum asked, "Where did you see your sprouts last?"

Jason thought. "On my windowsill," he said.

"*After* that," said Stacy.

Jason thought some more. "Beats me."

"Well, think!" Eric said.

Jason felt nervous. He looked around the room at his friends. "Do you know something I don't?" he asked.

All of them nodded.

Jason jumped up and down. "You've found my sprouts?"

Eric pointed to the kitchen. "Look! I can see them from here."

Jason whirled around. He stared straight ahead. Eric was right! The sprouts were in plain sight—on top of the refrigerator. Right where Stacy had put them.

Jason raced to the kitchen. He dragged a chair across the floor.

Zoom! He dashed back into the living room. His friends were smiling. Really smiling.

Jason stood there holding his sprouts. His stomach was in knots. "I'm sorry," he began. "I did a horrible thing . . . putting the cheese in your sneakers."

Dunkum went to stand beside Jason. "That's okay."

Eric frowned. "That's easy for *you* to say," he told Dunkum. "You don't have stinky sneakers!"

"*I* forgive Jason," Abby said. She came over and looked at his sprouts. "We stick together around here, remember?"

Shawn nodded. He ran around hugging all the kids.

Jason grinned.

Twelve

The next day, the Cul-de-Sac Kids hurried to Blossom Hill School. Together.

When Miss Hershey saw Jason with his sprouts, she clapped.

"Look who found his project," Abby said.

Miss Hershey smelled the bright green alfalfa sprouts. "Mm-m. Could I pay you to grow some for me?" she asked Jason.

"Sounds good." Jason looked at Eric and Shawn. He looked at Abby and Stacy. "I need to buy some new sneakers for my friends," he said.

Eric smiled. But not that sly smile.

Jason danced a jig to the science fair table. He put his sprouts on display.

Abby offered to water them. Eric straightened the plastic under the carpet.

Jason stepped back for a long look.

Then he knew. First place didn't matter anymore. Not really.

■ ■ ■

Later that day, the judges came to Miss Hershey's class. The first-place ribbon was big and blue. It had shiny gold letters on it.

The judge placed it next to Eric's fingerprint experiment. Eric had won. He deserved first place!

The class cheered. Especially Jason.

"Eric . . . Eric . . ." Jason started the chant.

The rest of the class joined in.

Eric's name flew all around the classroom.

And Jason was glad.

BOOK 8

Pickle Pizza

For
Matt Whiteis,
my pickle-lovin' fan.

One

Eric Hagel was flat broke.

He sat in the dugout with his buddy Dunkum Mifflin. Eric shoved his bat into the dirt. "Only two days till Father's Day," he said.

"Two days—and I can't wait." Dunkum thumped his fist into his catcher's mitt. "My dad's gonna be so surprised."

Eric was silent.

Dunkum kept talking. "I bought a giant crossword-puzzle book. My dad has a puzzle habit, you know."

Eric nodded. "Did you buy it with your own money?"

"I saved up for a couple of weeks," Dunkum said.

Eric wished he had money of his own. He wanted to buy a Father's Day present for his grandpa who lived with them.

There wasn't much money to go around. His mom baked special-order cakes for extra money. Grandpa repaired watches, but his eyes weren't strong anymore. He worked only three afternoons a week.

"What about you?" Dunkum asked. "Have you been saving up?"

"Not much. My paper-route money goes to the family," Eric answered. He'd had the route for a whole year. But there never seemed to be money left over. At least not enough for a Father's Day present.

"Are you going to celebrate with your grandpa?" Dunkum asked.

Eric smiled. "He's been kinda like a father to me since my dad died. There's only one thing . . ."

"What's that?" Dunkum asked.

"I'm broke. I can't buy anything."

Dunkum stood up. "Why don't you make something?"

Jason Birchall walked up to them. "Make what? What are we talking about?"

Eric shrugged his shoulders. "Father's Day. Dunkum thinks I should make something for Grandpa."

"Sure, why not?" Jason said. "Some of the other Cul-de-Sac Kids are making things."

Dunkum nodded. "Abby Hunter always says, 'Homemade gifts are the best.'"

Eric got up and swung his bat around. "Sounds good. But *what*? What can I make?"

Eric, Dunkum, and Jason made a huddle. A think huddle.

"What does your grandpa like?" Dunkum asked.

Eric thought a moment. "Birds. He's bird-crazy."

Jason started laughing.

Eric frowned. "What's so funny?"

"I saw him spying on a bird's nest yesterday," Jason replied. "He was up on his step stool—wearing those weird field glasses."

"They're *not* weird," Eric said. "They come in handy sometimes." He was thinking about last Christmas. Grandpa's field glasses had helped solve a mystery. "Remember those crazy Christmas angels next door?" Eric asked. "At Mr. Tressler's house?"

"Hey, you're right!" Jason said, laughing. "Remember those Christmas cookies Dee Dee and Carly made?"

Dunkum's eyes lit up. "And Stacy made a card with gold glitter. Remember that?"

"Hey! I have an idea," Jason said. "Why don't you ask Stacy about her art class?"

Eric's mouth pinched up. "Why should I?"

"Because Stacy's a good artist," Dunkum said. "Maybe she'll give you some ideas for Father's Day."

"Or maybe she'll take you to art class with her," Jason said. He danced around like it was a big deal.

Eric shook his head. "How can I get her to invite me?"

Jason laughed. "Just ask her, silly. She doesn't bite."

Eric's face got red. "I know that."

"Then ask her," Jason teased.

Eric scratched his head. "I'll think about it."

Two

E ric ate supper fast.

It was still light out when he finished. He dashed across the street to Stacy Henry's house.

She opened the door. "Hi," Stacy said.

"Hi," Eric said back. He didn't know what else to say.

"What do you want?" she asked.

"Oh . . . uh, nothing." Then he remembered what Dunkum said. "I heard you were making something."

Stacy's face burst into a grin. "I'm working on a gift for my dad—for Father's Day."

"Oh." The rest of the words got stuck in Eric's throat. The words he couldn't speak.

"My dad's coming on Sunday," she said. "I haven't seen him since Easter."

Eric remembered. The Cul-de-Sac Kids had surprised their parents with an Easter pet parade. Stacy's dad had come to see it, too.

"I'm glad about your dad," Eric said.

She nodded. "I can't wait. I really miss him."

Eric understood. He missed his dad, too.

"What are you making?" Eric asked.

Stacy opened the door. "Come in. I'll show you."

Eric followed Stacy downstairs. They went through the family room and into a smaller room.

"This is my new art room," Stacy said. "My mom and I just finished it."

Eric looked around.

An easel stood at one end of the room with paints and brushes. Drawings hung on the wall. "Wow," Eric said. "This is really great."

"It used to be a storage room," Stacy explained. "My mom decided I should have a place to work."

Eric spotted a lump of green clay on the worktable. "What's that?" he asked.

"Just some practice clay. But look what else I'm sculpting." She opened a cabinet door. Stacy reached in and pulled out a small eagle sculpture. She held it high. "What do you think?"

"It's terrific!" Eric couldn't believe his eyes.

Stacy smiled. "I hope Daddy likes it."

"I'm sure he will," Eric said.

Stacy smiled and set the eagle down.

Eric crept over to Stacy's worktable. He studied the eagle. The eagle was facing straight ahead. The wings were up, as if the bird was ready to fly. "What's it made of?" Eric asked.

"Sculpey."

"What's that?" Eric asked.

"It's like soft clay. You bake it in the oven, and it gets hard. When it cools off, you can paint it."

"Wow," Eric whispered. He wished he could make something like this for Grandpa.

"Here, feel it," Stacy said.

Eric reached out with his pointer finger. Gently, he touched the eagle's head. "It feels smooth. No bumps or lumps."

Stacy nodded. "Thanks. I worked hard."

72

Eric stood up. He looked at Stacy. *Should I ask about going to her art class?* he wondered.

"What are you staring at?" Stacy asked.

Eric looked away. "I . . . uh . . . oh, nothing."

Father's Day was coming fast. Would Stacy invite him to art class?

Eric hoped so. He *really* hoped so.

Three

Eric couldn't stop thinking about the art class.

"I wonder if—" He stopped.

Stacy blinked her eyes. "What do you wonder?"

Eric tried again. "I . . . er . . . Argh!" The words didn't want to come out. Not the ones he wanted to say.

Stacy's eyes grew wide.

At last, Eric said, "I like your eagle sculpture. Thanks for showing me."

Stacy grinned. "Anytime."

"Well, see ya," Eric said.

Stacy walked upstairs with him. "Thanks for coming," she said.

"Good-bye." The screen door slapped shut behind him.

Eric clumped down the sidewalk. He wished he'd asked about the art class. He wished he weren't so shy sometimes.

Zippo! A flash of green leaped past him. Something green with skinny legs.

Jason's frog, Croaker, was loose!

Eric chased after the bullfrog. "Come back!" he called.

> Croaker
> hopped
> all
> the
> way
> down
> Blossom Hill Lane.

Eric ran after the frog. "Croaker, come back!"

Boink! The frog leaped into a bush in front of Dunkum's house. Out of sight.

Eric got down on his knees. He pushed the branches back. But Croaker was out of reach.

"What are you doing in there, Croaker?" Eric called.

Suddenly, he heard footsteps. Eric turned around.

It was Jason Birchall.

"Who are you talking to?" Jason asked.

"To your frog." Eric pointed to the bush. "He disappeared in there."

Jason leaned down and peered into the bush.

"How'd he get loose?" Eric asked.

"Your grandpa came over to borrow some sugar. He wanted to see my frog up close," Jason explained. "So I took Croaker out of the aquarium."

Eric scratched his head. "My grandpa wanted to see your frog?"

"Yep." Jason stood up and brushed off his jeans. "And he said something really weird."

"Like what?" Eric asked.

"'Frogs and pickles look alike.'" Jason laughed.

"Hey, don't make fun."

Jason poked playfully at Eric. "Frogs and pickles *do* have something in common."

"Yeah. They're both green," Eric said. "And they have bumps."

Jason pushed up his glasses. "How do frogs taste?"

Eric laughed out loud. "That's gross! But some *pickles* are sweet. My favorite!"

"Not me," Jason said. "I like dill pickles."

"So does my grandpa." Eric thought about Father's Day again. "Are you making something for your dad?"

"First, I have to find my frog." Jason inched around the bush, looking.

"Well, good luck finding your four-legged pickle," Eric teased.

Frogs and pickles. Grandpa should do stand-up comedy!

Quickly, Eric headed up the cul-de-sac. He wanted to stop by Stacy's house again.

He stuck out his chin. *This* time he'd get brave. He would invite himself to Stacy's art class.

It was now or never!

Four

Eric ran up the steps to Stacy's house.

He could see inside the screen door. Sunday Funnies wagged his fluffy tail.

"Hey there, boy," Eric said.

The white cockapoo always found the Sunday comics first. That's why he had such a silly name.

Sunday Funnies yipped and jumped up.

Eric hoped Stacy would hear her puppy. He wanted her to come to the door so he wouldn't have to knock.

Seconds passed, but Stacy didn't come.

Eric decided to knock. A soft, shy knock. The screen door flapped gently against the frame.

He waited.

Sunday Funnies kept barking and running around. He wanted to play.

At last, Stacy came to the door.

Eric stood tall. "Hi again."

"Hi." She stared at him.

Eric felt silly. He looked down at his sneakers.

"What's wrong?" Stacy asked.

"Uh . . . nothing."

"Really?" she said.

"It's just . . ." He was having trouble saying it.

"Why don't you say what you're thinking?" Stacy opened the screen door and came outside.

OK, here goes, Eric thought. He took a deep breath. "Can I go to your art class tomorrow?"

"*Can* you?" There was a twinkle in her eye. "I don't know if you can."

"I can't?" Eric asked.

Stacy frowned. "Are you allowed to come?"

"Allowed?" Eric was mixed up.

"Yeah, did you ask your mom?"

Eric shook his head. "Not yet."

"Well, the correct way to ask is, '*May* I go with you?'"

Eric sat on the front step.

"Just remember, *can* means able to," Stacy said. "*May* means allowed to."

Eric sighed. He hadn't expected a language lesson.

"OK," Stacy said, smiling. "That's settled." She pulled a piece of green bubble gum out of her pocket. "Want some?"

"Sure, thanks." Eric stuffed the gum in his mouth.

Stacy opened a piece of pink bubble gum for herself.

"I want to make a bird tomorrow," Eric said. "What's the name of that stuff again?"

"Sculpey."

Eric smiled. "That's what I'm going to use."

"Good choice," she said.

Whammo! Eric socked the air.

Now he felt good.

Just then, Eric spotted Jason across the street. He had Croaker between both hands. And he was running.

"Hey, Jason!" Eric called to him.

Jason glanced over his shoulder. "I finally caught my frog. It took all this time." Then he hurried into his house.

Eric blew a giant green bubble. He thought about Grandpa wanting to see Croaker up close. And he thought about Father's Day.

His sculpting project was going to be perfect. Eric couldn't wait to get started.

I'll have to work hard, he thought. *Father's Day is almost here!*

Five

It was Saturday. At last!

Eric delivered the newspapers extra early. Extra fast.

When he was finished, he came home and took a shower. Then he dressed for art class.

Eric tiptoed into Grandpa's room.

Z-z-z-srnnk! The snoring shook the old bed.

Eric crept past the dresser. Past the closet. He peeked into Grandpa's bookcase.

Good! The bird book was there. Eric slid it under his arm. He would borrow it for the class.

■ ■ ■

Stacy was waiting outside when Eric arrived. She was holding a small box. Her unpainted eagle was inside.

Eric showed her the bird book.

"Wow," she said. "This is cool."

They sat on the step looking at the book. Stacy turned the pages carefully. "What bright colors! And the pictures are so big."

"Grandpa likes them that way."

Stacy said softly, "I hope his eyes get better."

"Me too," Eric said. "Grandpa wears a magnifying glass when he repairs watches. But not when he's looking at this book."

Stacy smiled. "He wears his field glasses for bird watching, too."

Eric smiled back. "Watching birds is his favorite thing. But his eyes are getting weak."

"Then your idea is perfect," she said. "Sculptures are great to touch. Even if your grandpa loses his sight, he'll be able to *feel* your bird!"

Eric hadn't thought of that.

Soon it was time to leave for art class. Stacy's mom was a careful driver. But Eric wished she would zoom around the corners.

To make the time pass, he studied the bird book.

At last, they arrived in front of a brick house. A white sign hung from the lamppost. It read *Young Artists' Studio.*

Stacy's mom waved good-bye and pulled away from the curb. Eric followed Stacy up the stony walkway.

"This is where I come every Saturday," she said. They went inside. Rows of sketches, cartoons, and paintings decorated the walls. A dark-haired lady sat behind a wide desk.

Stacy went up to the desk. "This is my friend Eric," she told the lady. "He's my guest today."

"Welcome." The desk lady smiled.

Stacy turned to Eric. "Eric, this is Miss Lana. She signs kids up for classes."

Eric grinned. "I'd like to sign up sometime."

"We'd love to have you," Miss Lana said.

Stacy and Eric headed down the hall. In the sculpting studio, Eric counted ten kids at work.

"Follow me," Stacy said. Her table was small, like all the others. A set of paints and some brushes were there.

Mr. Albert came over. "Nice to see you, Stacy," her teacher said.

Stacy introduced Eric. "Eric's one of the Cul-de-Sac Kids. It's a club." She explained about the seven houses on their block. "We have nine kids on Blossom Hill Lane. Most of us are making something for Father's Day."

Eric listened.

Stacy continued. "Eric wants to make a bird out of Sculpey." She didn't say it was for his grandpa. Maybe she didn't want to say that Eric's dad had died.

Eric looked at her. *Stacy's a good friend*, he thought.

The teacher scooted a table next to Stacy's. He found an extra chair. "There we are," said Mr. Albert. "I will be glad to help you, Eric."

"Thanks." Eric showed him the bird book and the picture of a red robin. The teacher gave him some basic pointers. Then he went to help another student.

Stacy got Eric started. She stuck her hands into his Sculpey. Right into the middle of it. She worked it like bread dough. "There, that's how to begin. Now *you* try."

Eric stared at the white clump. He picked

it up. The Sculpey felt cool in his hands. And a little hard.

Smash! He jammed it between his hands.

Stacy grinned. "That's it!"

Eric glanced at Stacy's eagle. What a beautiful sculpture—the smooth body and graceful wings.

He stared at his blob of nothing.

Eric's stomach flip-flopped.

Beside him, Stacy began to paint. He watched her work. Then he looked down at his table. *Ee-yew*, he thought. *This glob is supposed to be a Father's Day present?*

Eric pulled his fingers out of the Sculpey. They were shaking. *What am I doing here?*

Six

Eric's heart was pounding.

He got up and left the room. He stood in the hallway.

Stacy rushed out. "What's wrong, Eric?"

He stared at the floor. "I don't belong here."

Stacy grabbed his arm. "You'll never know if you don't try."

Eric knew she was right. "What if it turns out all yucky?" he asked.

Stacy said, "Just do your best. That's what counts."

Eric agreed to try again.

He went back into the classroom with Stacy. He walked past young artists. He saw their small statues. Dolphins, lions, a clown, and even a T-rex. These were works in progress.

Eric sat at his table and took a deep breath. He picked up the bird book and flipped through the pages. The red robin picture was on page 33.

With his finger, he traced the lines of its round shape. He was ready to form the body. Next came the tiny head and wings.

Eric worked for two hours. Several times, Mr. Albert came to help and give advice. Stacy helped, too.

By the end of class, Eric's work was only half finished. He frowned. "Tomorrow's Father's Day. I can't give this mess to my grandpa."

Stacy said, "Just tell him you're working on a top-secret project. When the sculpture's done, give it to him."

Eric shook his head. "It might take weeks. I want something for *tomorrow*!"

"What's wrong with giving him the unfinished robin?" she asked.

"I just told you." Eric put his robin glob in a box. "It isn't done."

Stacy wiggled her nose. Off she went to clean up her work area.

Mr. Albert stopped by. Eric thanked him for his help.

"Perhaps you can join us," Mr. Albert suggested.

"I'd like that," Eric said. But he knew it was impossible. Besides, he wasn't an artist.

Eric went outside to wait for Stacy. He gripped his cardboard box. On top of it, he carried the bird book. Inside the box was a blobby, globby robin.

One after another, the young artists came with their sculptures. Eric tried not to stare.

If only my sculpture were finished! he thought. *If only I could come to class like Stacy all the time.*

Father's Day tomorrow—and no present. Eric felt sorry for his grandpa.

He felt sorry for himself, too.

Seven

*H*onk! *Honk!*

Eric and Stacy ran to get in the car.

"How was art class?" Stacy's mother asked.

Stacy glanced at Eric. "I finished painting my eagle."

Eric slumped down in the back seat. The bird book lay on the seat beside him.

"What about you, Eric?" Stacy's mother asked.

"I . . . uh, it was nice." Eric thought about the class. Mr. Albert and Miss Lana. Stacy and the other kids. All of them had been very nice.

The NOT nice thing was in his box. The yucko bird sculpture!

Eric put the box on the floor—and stuck his tongue out at it.

Stacy and her mom were talking in the front seat. They were making Father's Day plans. They were planning how to gift wrap the eagle sculpture.

Eric slapped his hands over his ears. He didn't want to hear about Father's Day. He didn't want to hear about Stacy's eagle.

A lump choked Eric's throat. He missed his dad.

But he had a terrific grandpa. Eric wanted him to know how special he was. Very special.

Sometimes at night, Eric would tiptoe down the hall. He'd peek into Grandpa's room and listen. In the darkness, he could hear Grandpa talking to God. "Please bless Eric, my grandson," Grandpa would say.

Those prayers made Eric feel good. And strong.

■■■

Stacy turned around in the front seat. Her eyes were kind.

Eric took his hands away from his ears.

"Are you OK?" Stacy asked.

Eric shrugged his shoulders.

Just then, Stacy's mom made a left turn. The box holding Eric's project slid toward the door. The unfinished bird rolled out. Eric kept his seat belt on. He stared at the bird.

When the car pulled into the driveway, Eric picked up his sculpture. Quickly, he scooped it into the box. He climbed out of the car. "Thanks for taking me."

"Remember what I told you," Stacy said. "You can finish your sculpture later. Then give it to your grandpa." Her voice was soft.

"I know," Eric said. But more than anything, he wanted something for tomorrow. Tomorrow was the day Grandpa deserved a special gift.

Eric closed the lid on the box and headed for home. Someday, he would finish the sculpture. Maybe for Grandpa's birthday. Or Christmas.

But *today,* he would think of something. Something to give Grandpa for Father's Day.

There was no time to waste!

Eight

Eric carried the box upstairs. He shoved it under his bed. Then he went to Grandpa's room to return the bird book.

Eric decided to go outside.

Carly Hunter was making chalk drawings on the sidewalk. Big, bright drawings.

Dee Dee Winters, Carly's best friend, came skating down the sidewalk.

"Hello, Eric!" Dee Dee called.

Eric wandered over to the girls. He stood there quietly with his hands in his pockets.

Carly looked up at him. "Aren't you talking?"

Eric shook his head. "Not much."

"How come?" Dee Dee asked.

"Long story," Eric said. He was thinking about Father's Day. Again.

Carly stood up. She put her arm around Dee Dee. "Well, maybe *we* can help."

Dee Dee agreed. "Yeah, we make a mean batch of cookies." She turned to Carly. "Baking cookies—and eating them—always helps if you're sad." Dee Dee's face burst into a big smile. "That's what we made for Father's Day gifts."

Whammo! An idea struck Eric.

His hands flew out of his pockets. "Got any recipe books?"

"Do I ever!" Dee Dee said.

"Can I borrow one?" Eric asked.

"You mean, *may* you?" Dee Dee said.

Eric smiled to himself. Another language lesson?

"Wait here!" Dee Dee skated down the street.

When she came back, Dee Dee showed off her favorite recipes.

Carly peered at the book, then at Eric. "Are *you* gonna bake cookies?"

Eric stared at the recipe book. He scratched his head. "Maybe."

Beep, beep! Dunkum and Jason came riding their bikes. "Look out!" yelled Jason.

Eric played along and acted scared. He jumped onto the sidewalk. Dunkum and Jason dropped their bikes on the grass.

"What's up?" asked Jason.

"Nothing much," Eric said.

Dunkum spotted the recipe book. "Are you making Father's Day cookies?" he asked Eric.

"I'm thinking about it," Eric said.

Dee Dee was still looking at her book. "Hey! Here are pizza recipes!"

"So?" Dunkum said.

"I *love* pizza!" Dee Dee said.

"Me too," Eric said. He went to look at the book again.

Carly put down her colored chalk. "Let's see how many pizza recipes are in there." She squeezed between Dee Dee and Eric to have a look.

While Carly counted, Eric's brain whirled. *Homemade pizza for Father's Day,* he thought. *What a great idea!*

■■■

After lunch, Eric read the pizza recipe. It was called "The Perfect Pizza."

Eric chuckled to himself. His pizza was going to be more than perfect. It was going to be a surprise.

The best Father's Day pizza ever!

Nine

Eric sat at the kitchen table. He opened Dee Dee's recipe book.

His mother dried her hands. "Looks like someone's going to cook," she said.

"I'm gonna try."

She leaned over his shoulder. "Mm-m, pizza. Good idea."

"Sh-h! It's a secret for Grandpa," Eric said. "For Father's Day."

"Need some help?" Mrs. Hagel's eyes twinkled. "I'm a pro, you know."

"You can help me," he said. "You can keep Grandpa out of the kitchen."

"It's a deal." She closed the kitchen door.

"Work in progress." Eric chuckled softly.

In the cupboard, he found the flour, salt,

and pepper. In the fridge, he found the eggs and milk.

Suddenly, he spotted the pickle jar.

Dill pickles!

Grandpa loved pickles. He ate pickles with everything. Scrambled eggs and pickles. Mashed potatoes and pickles. Broccoli, peas, and carrots—all with pickles. He even ate pickles with apple pie!

Eric grabbed the pickle jar. "My pizza *will* be perfect," he said out loud. "A perfect pickle pizza!"

Quickly, he set to work. He grated the cheese. Lots of it. Next, he made the dough for the crust. After that, Eric opened a can of pizza sauce.

Then he chopped the pickles on the cutting board. *What a great topping*, he thought as he chopped.

Thirty minutes later, the pizza was ready for topping. Eric took it out of the oven. He sprinkled on extra cheese and pizza sauce. And piles of chopped pickles.

Then he slid the pan back into the oven. The timer was set. Ten minutes to go.

Soon, the smell of hot dill filled the kitchen. He couldn't wait to taste his perfect pizza.

Buzz-zing! The timer went off.

Eric removed the pan from the oven. Carefully, he cut ten pieces.

Tap, tap. Someone knocked on the back door.

He hurried to open it.

There stood Carly and Dee Dee with a plateful of cookies. "Hi again," Carly said, giggling.

Eric gazed at the cookies.

"We're having a taste test," Dee Dee said. "Help yourself."

"Thanks!" Eric bit into a chocolate chip cookie. "Mm-m, it's great!"

"Goody!" said Carly.

Dee Dee sniffed the air. "Hey, what's that smell?"

"My Father's Day pizza," Eric said.

Carly wrinkled her nose. "It smells . . . uh, funny."

Then Eric had an idea. "Wait here," he said and raced back inside.

In a flash, he was back with his pickle pizza. "Who wants to taste *my* baking?" he asked.

Dee Dee crept up to the pizza. Her eyes got very big. "What's in it?"

"Just taste it," Eric insisted.

"Uh . . . I don't know," Carly said.

Carly and Dee Dee stared at the pizza.

"You go first," Dee Dee said to Carly.

"No, *you*," Carly said.

Eric stepped between them. He handed each girl a piece of pizza. "Here. Taste it together," he said. "On your mark, get set . . . bite!"

Carly and Dee Dee bit into Eric's pickle pizza. They coughed and spit it out.

Dee Dee began to gag. "This is gross!"

Eric's heart sank. *My pizza is a flop!*

He snatched up the pizza and ran into the house.

Back inside, Eric wrapped up the pizza slices. He shoved them way back in the fridge. Maybe he'd feed Grandpa's birds tomorrow. *If* he could get them to eat pickle pizza pieces!

Feeling sad, Eric went to his room. He looked at the calendar beside his bed. Saturday, June 15. Father's Day was almost here. There was nothing to give Grandpa.

Time had run out.

Ten

The Hagels went to church the next day. Eric sat between his grandpa and mother.

After church, Eric helped set the dining room table. He went to the kitchen for some napkins. That's when he saw Grandpa poking around in the fridge.

"What's this?" Grandpa held up a slice of cold pizza.

"Nothing you'd want to eat," Eric said.

Grandpa unwrapped a slice. "Are you sure?"

"It's terrible. It's—" Eric stopped.

"What's wrong with it?"

Eric stared at the floor. "It was supposed to

be your Father's Day present. But it turned out yucky. I'm real sorry."

Grandpa touched Eric's shoulder. "It's the thought that counts."

"Maybe the birds will eat it," Eric said.

Grandpa didn't answer. He took a dish out of the cupboard. But his eyes were on the pizza.

Then he put the pizza in the microwave to reheat.

What's he doing? Eric wondered.

He remembered yesterday's taste test. Dee Dee and Carly had hated his pizza. They'd even spit it out!

The timer bell rang. The pizza was warm. Grandpa blew on it gently. Then he bit into the pickle pizza.

Eric held his breath. Would Grandpa gag, too?

There was a long silence.

Then Grandpa's face lit up. "This is wonderful! Simply wonderful!"

Eric couldn't believe his ears. Or his eyes! "You like it?" he asked.

Grandpa's face wrinkled up in the biggest smile ever. "This is a *grand* Father's Day present!"

Eric hugged him. "Really?"

"You know I love pickles." Grandpa was grinning.

Eric's mother came into the kitchen. She was carrying the box from art class.

Eric rushed over to her. He whispered, "Where'd you find that?"

"Under your bed," she said. "I was looking for your shoes and there it was."

Eric's eyes darted to Grandpa. He pulled his mom out of the kitchen. "I don't want Grandpa to know about this yet," he explained. "It's a sculpting project."

She smiled. "I can see that. And I want you to finish it."

"Someday." Eric closed the lid.

"How about this summer?" she said. "Mr. Albert called yesterday."

"From the art studio?" Eric asked.

She nodded. "He wants to give you a grant for art lessons."

"He's going to *pay* for my art classes?"

"Are you interested?" she asked.

"Are pickles green?" Eric hugged his mother.

"That must be a yes," she said.

Grandpa peeked his head around the corner. "Why all the whispering?"

Eric's mother told him the exciting news. She told Grandpa without saying a word about the robin in the box. The robin that was waiting to be finished.

"Well, what do you know! We have an artist in the house." Grandpa winked at Eric. "And a wonderful chef!"

Eric stood tall. And reached for a slice of pickle pizza.

BOOK 9

Mailbox Mania

To
Kendra Verhage,
my talented young cousin.
Someday, I hope to see your
stories in print!

One

Abby Hunter yawned and stretched. And yawned again.

Summer had come. Hot, fly-buzzin' summer.

No school. Nothing to do.

Abby missed school. She missed her favorite teacher, Miss Hershey. "Summer's boring," Abby said to her sister, Carly.

Carly crabbed about her paper dolls. "They're floppy," she said.

Their adopted Korean brothers, Shawn and Jimmy, were tired of American rice. "It's too dry," they said.

All the Cul-de-Sac Kids were bored.

Dunkum Mifflin boxed up his basketball. "Too hot to play," he said.

Stacy Henry was sick of sculpting. "The clay's too soft when it's hot outside," she said.

Jason Birchall fussed about his frog. "Croaker never says *ribbit* anymore."

Eric Hagel complained about his paper route. "I never get to sleep in."

But the Fourth of July was coming. The United States of America's birthday.

Abby and her friends stood in front of her house. "Four more days," she said. "I can't wait!"

Eric and Dunkum, Stacy and Shawn agreed.

The younger Cul-de-Sac Kids looked at each other. Dee Dee, Carly, and Jimmy shrugged their shoulders. "We oughta have a club meeting," Dee Dee said.

"Good idea," Abby said. She was the president of the Cul-de-Sac Kids. Nine kids who lived on one street.

Dunkum smiled. "Let's meet at my house."

Abby grinned. They *always* met at Dunkum's

house. He had the biggest basement. "How soon?" asked Abby.

"Give me ten minutes to straighten things up," said Dunkum. And he jogged down the cul-de-sac.

Carly, Dee Dee, and the others crowded around Abby.

"Let's think up something to do," Jason said. "Something really fun!"

"Yeah," Eric said. "Let's brainstorm."

Stacy leaned on Abby's mailbox. "I can't think of anything fun."

Abby tried to dream up something.

Just then, a mail truck came down the street. Mr. Pete, the postal worker, stopped at each house. The kids watched him till he came to Abby's house.

Mr. Pete waved to them. "Good morning, kids!"

The Cul-de-Sac Kids waved, too.

Stacy backed away from the mailbox. Mr. Pete stuffed the Hunter mailbox full.

Abby stared at the mailbox. Then an idea hit. "I know!" she shouted. "I know what we can do!"

Carly spun around. "What?"

"Tell us!" Jason said.

Dee Dee's eyes got big. "Please?"

"Come on," Abby said. "It's time for our meeting. I'll tell you about it there."

And she raced down the cul-de-sac to Dunkum's.

TWO

Abby took off her sneakers. They were new. One red, one blue.

The kids lined up their sneakers along the wall.

Jason plopped down on the floor. The others did, too. "Okay," Jason said. "Let's get started."

Abby sat in the president's seat—a beanbag. "The meeting will come to order," she said. "Does anyone have old business?"

"Forget the old business," Jason hollered. "Let's have the new stuff!"

"Tell us your idea, Abby!" Carly shouted. "We can't wait!"

Soon, all the Cul-de-Sac Kids were shouting.

Dunkum whistled.

Quickly, they settled down.

"Now," Abby began. "Let's start over."

Eric's eyes shone. "Abby sounds like a teacher."

Abby grinned. She liked that. Maybe someday she'd be a teacher like Miss Hershey.

Jason swayed back and forth. He seemed wound up. "Forget school," he said. "Let's hear Abby's idea."

"Yahoo!" Dee Dee said.

Abby's voice grew soft. "I have a great Fourth-of-July idea."

The kids leaned forward, listening.

"A contest," she said. "We'll call it Mailbox Mania."

Eric yelled, "What's *that* mean?"

"Sh-h!" said Dee Dee. "Just listen."

"We'll decorate our mailboxes for our country's birthday," Abby said. "With American themes. Whatever you want."

"How about Paul Revere's horse?" Jason stood up and trotted around.

The kids laughed. But Dunkum pulled him back down.

"Someone can judge our mailboxes," Abby said. "The best mailbox wins."

Jimmy raised his hand. "I judge! I good judge."

Abby smiled. "Maybe it should be a grown-up."

Dunkum suggested someone. "How about Mr. Tressler?"

"Let's take a vote," Abby said. "How many want Mr. Tressler to judge the mailbox contest?"

Hands flew up.

"Double dabble good," Abby said. "Mr. Tressler's the one."

Shawn stared at Abby. "Who will decorate Hunter family mailbox? Four kids in family," he said in broken English.

"Good question," Abby said. "Any ideas?"

Eric raised his hand. "The four of you should work together. What's so hard about that?"

The rest of the kids agreed.

Abby glanced around. "Every Cul-de-Sac Kid except Carly, Jimmy, Shawn, and me is an only child. So the Hunter family will work together."

Shawn and Jimmy clapped. "Yippee!"

Carly frowned. "That's too many kids for *one* mailbox. Way too many!"

Abby hoped her sister was wrong about that. She hoped with all her heart.

Three

After lunch, they got started planning. Abby and Shawn, Carly and Jimmy Hunter.

They sat in the backyard under a shade tree. They sipped on lemonade and played with Snow White, their dog.

Abby began, "How should we decorate our mailbox?"

None of them knew.

"Any ideas?" She waited for her sister and brothers to respond.

None of them did.

"Don't we want to win the contest?" she asked.

Carly pouted. "You're the president of the

Cul-de-Sac Kids, *not* the president of the Hunter family."

Now it was Abby's turn to frown. "Why'd you say *that*?"

Shawn shook his head. "This not working."

"Just a minute!" Abby snapped. "Remember what Eric said? We have to work together."

"Good luck," Carly muttered.

"Let's choose a theme for our mailbox," Abby said.

Shawn looked puzzled. "Like what?"

Abby thought. "The Statue of Liberty?"

"Too hard," Carly said.

"We can try," Shawn said. He smiled at Abby. "I will try."

Carly shook her head. "Dumb idea."

"Don't say dumb," Abby replied.

"You're not the boss!" Carly stomped across the lawn. She sat on the back porch step.

Jimmy climbed a tree. "No contest for Hunter kids," he said.

Snow White barked up at him.

Shawn told Jimmy to come down. He said it in Korean. Abby could tell he was mad. "We cannot plan this way," he said. He glared up at Jimmy.

"I stay up here," Jimmy shouted. "I not come down!"

Abby felt like a jitterbug. She reached for her notebook and pencil. And her lemonade. Then she stood up.

"Where you go?" Shawn asked her.

Abby brushed off her shorts. "Maybe you're right. This won't work."

"But we try . . . and try," Shawn replied.

Abby glanced toward the house. Carly was pouting on the porch.

Abby stared at the tree. Jimmy was hanging upside down. "Looks like two against two," she said.

Shawn nodded. "We find a way," he said. "You see."

"I don't know." Abby sighed. "Maybe they should have Mailbox Mania without us."

Shawn's eyes were kind. "You say, 'Cul-de-Sac Kids stick together,' well . . . Hunter family do, too."

Abby sat down in the grass. She wanted to feel good about Mailbox Mania. She really wanted to.

But how could she when her family was fighting?

Four

The next day, Abby got up early.

She read her Bible. And prayed. "Dear Lord, help Carly and Jimmy. They aren't trying very hard to win the contest. Help us work together. Amen."

At breakfast, Carly ate her pancakes with too much syrup. Even Mother noticed.

Jimmy slurped his milk. The sound bugged Abby. "Where are your manners?" she said.

"Where are yours?" he shot back.

"Children, please," said Abby's mother.

Shawn was the only quiet one. Abby wished she had just one brother and no sister. Jimmy and Carly could go fly a kite!

Abby and Shawn helped clean up the kitchen. Then Abby went to Stacy's house.

"Let's go swimming," Abby suggested.

"Can't," Stacy said. "I'm working on my mailbox."

"Oh yeah. Lucky you!" Abby turned to go. She was heading home when Mr. Tressler came outside. He was swinging his cane as he walked.

"Hello there, missy," Mr. Tressler called to her.

Abby waved. She ran across the street. "Can I talk to you?"

He smiled his wrinkled smile. "You're talking, aren't you?"

Abby explained all about Mailbox Mania. "We need a judge," she said. "Someone who can be fair."

He leaned on his cane. "Hm-m, sounds interesting."

"Do you want the job?"

He rubbed his pointy chin. "What's the pay?"

"Very funny," Abby said.

Mr. Tressler's eyes twinkled. "I'd be honored, Abby. When's the big day?"

"The Fourth of July."

"I'll be there with bells on."

Bells on? Abby wondered. Then she saw his smile and knew what he meant. "Thank you!"

Mr. Tressler waved his cane.

Abby felt good about Mr. Tressler doing the judging. But she wondered about her own mailbox. Could she get Carly and Jimmy to work on it? Would it be done in time?

The contest was only three days away!

"Maybe Shawn and I'll decorate by ourselves," she said out loud. Excited, she rushed across the street—to her side of the cul-de-sac.

At that moment, Stacy came out of her house. She carried a shoebox full of paints, paper, glue, and scissors. An eager look spread across her face.

Abby waved to her. "Hi, Stacy!"

Stacy froze.

"What's wrong?" Abby asked.

Stacy hid the shoebox behind her back. "I . . . uh . . . I didn't want you to see this."

Abby frowned. "Why not?"

"Well, I—" Stacy stopped.

"What?" Abby had a weird feeling.

"You won't steal my idea, will you?" Stacy asked.

Abby held her breath. She didn't say a word.

"Well, you won't, will you?" Stacy said.

Abby folded her arms across her chest. "You know me better than that, Stacy Henry!"

And she ran home.

Five

That night, Abby couldn't sleep.

Crackity boom! Early fireworks.

Something else kept her awake. Starting tomorrow, there were only two days left. The Fourth of July—and Mailbox Mania—was coming fast!

It was late when Abby fell asleep. Her dreams popped with the sounds outside. In one dream, Jason was making popcorn in his mailbox. The hot sun beat down.

Ka-bang! The mailbox exploded into a giant popcorn ball.

Abby woke up caught in her covers. Too hot. She kicked them off and went back to sleep.

■■■

The next morning, Abby crept into Carly's room. Her closet door stood open. Carly was humming.

Inside the closet was a secret place. The sliding door led to a tiny space under the steps.

"Ps-st! Are you in there?" Abby called.

The humming stopped.

Rustle rattle.

Then—"Keep out!" Carly shouted.

Abby caught a glimpse of her sister. She was working on something. Probably something for Mailbox Mania.

Abby inched closer. "What are you doing?"

Carly hid whatever she was making. "Go away!"

"We have to talk," Abby said.

"*I'm* not talking. And that's final."

Abby sighed. "I know what you're doing, and it's not fair. We have to work together."

"Nope," Carly said. "I'm making my own mailbox creation. And you can't stop me!"

Abby stared.

Carly pouted.

"Fine," Abby said at last. "We'll have Mailbox Mania without you." And she turned to go.

"Mommy!" Carly yelled.

Abby shook her head as she hurried outside. *Such a baby!* she thought.

Across the street, Eric was working on his mailbox.

Abby watched him from her front porch. It looked like he was using green clay. A clay sculpture!

She stood up for a better look. It was the lady with the lamp, all right. The Statue of Liberty!

Just then, Jason ran over to Eric. Abby could see what was happening. Jason and Eric were arguing.

"You copied my idea!" Jason hollered.

Eric shrugged his shoulders. "How was I supposed to know?"

"Well, I won't let you make it!" Jason shouted. He leaped toward the Lady of Liberty.

Abby gasped. "No!"

But it was too late. Eric's clay sculpture fell to the ground.

Abby felt sick. This wasn't Mailbox Mania at all! It was a Mailbox Mess!

Six

Abby dashed across the street. "Let me help," she said.

Eric didn't say a word.

Abby could hear his short, quick breaths.

"What an awful thing," she said. "I can't believe Jason did this!"

Eric carried his clay pieces inside.

Next door, Mr. Tressler sat on his porch. His face looked very sad. As sad as Abby felt.

She stormed up to Jason's house. Mrs. Birchall came to the door. Abby wanted to tell on Jason. But she didn't. "May I speak to Jason, please?"

Mrs. Birchall nodded. "I'll get him."

In a few minutes, she returned. Without

Jason. "I'm sorry," she said. "I can't seem to find him."

Abby knew why. Jason was hiding!

"I'll talk to him later," she said. "Thank you." And down the cul-de-sac she ran—to Dunkum's.

Dunkum Mifflin would know what to do. He always did.

When she got there, Dee Dee Winters was ringing his doorbell. Her face looked like a prune. "I quit," she said.

"You what?"

"I'm quitting the mailbox contest," Dee Dee insisted.

Abby looked at the little girl. "What's wrong?"

"Everything."

Dunkum came to the door. "Hi," he said. "What's up?"

"You busy?" Dee Dee asked him.

"Kinda," he said.

"Don't tell me," she said. "You're working on your mailbox?"

Dunkum looked puzzled. "Isn't everyone?"

Dee Dee shook her head. "I'm not."

"Well, why not?" Dunkum smiled. "Need some help?"

"Now you're talking!" Dee Dee's face lit up.

Dunkum looked at Abby. "Is it okay? If I help her, I mean?"

"Don't ask me." Abby took two steps backward.

"You're the Cul-de-Sac Kids' president, aren't you?" he said.

Abby studied Dee Dee. She *was* only seven. Then she thought of her sister—Dee Dee's best friend.

"What if Carly finds out?" Abby said. "That might cause trouble."

"There already *is* trouble," Dunkum said.

Abby took two steps forward. "What do you mean?"

Dunkum's face twitched. "Maybe you should ask your sister."

"What's wrong with Carly?" Abby asked. But she already knew. Her own sister was making things hard. And horrible.

For everyone!

Seven

Abby called a meeting.

Stacy, Dunkum, and Shawn showed up.

"Where is everyone else?" Stacy asked.

Abby explained. "We have some problems. Carly and Jimmy are mad at me. Jason and Eric are fighting. And Dee Dee asked Dunkum for help."

"Why should Dee Dee get help?" Stacy asked.

"She's little, that's why," Dunkum said.

Stacy shook her head.

Abby was worried. Would Dunkum and Stacy start arguing, too? "What should we do?" she asked. "Do we need to vote about Dee Dee or what?"

Dunkum looked around. "There aren't enough members here."

Shawn agreed. "Only four kids."

"Well," Stacy huffed. "What's Dee Dee making that's so hard?"

Dunkum spoke up. "She's making an Abe Lincoln mailbox. With a top hat and beard."

"You're kidding," Stacy said. "She should've asked *me*! I'm the artist on the block."

"But *I* live closer," Dunkum insisted.

Stacy's eyes were tiny slits. "That doesn't mean anything!" She got up and hurried down the street—to Dee Dee's.

"Hey! Wait!" Dunkum called.

But Stacy kept going.

"Well," Abby said, "I guess that's the end of our meeting."

"Cul-de-Sac Kids do *not* stick together. Not anymore," Shawn said. His eyes looked sad.

Dunkum left without saying good-bye.

Abby didn't know what to think. Were the Cul-de-Sac Kids falling apart?

She sat on the swing next to Shawn. "Now what?"

"In Korea, we talk to wise people," Shawn

said. "Older people—like grandfather or grandmother—are wise."

Abby thought of someone like that. "Maybe Mr. Tressler can help. He's old and wise!" She looked at Shawn. "You're a great brother!"

Shawn smiled. "Abby great sister . . . and friend."

Then Abby hurried to the house at the end of the cul-de-sac.

Could Mr. Tressler help?

Abby would find out soon enough!

Eight

bby ran to Mr. Tressler's house.

The old gentleman was having a snooze.

He snored softly, slumped down in his chair.

Abby crept up the porch steps and sat down. *I'll wait here till he wakes up*, she thought.

While she sat, she remembered happier days. Lots of happy days.

Not long ago, the Cul-de-Sac Kids were getting along. They'd made Father's Day gifts. And had an Easter pet parade. They'd even solved a mystery—*The Crazy Christmas Angel Mystery*.

Best of all, they were true friends.

But something had gone wrong. Crazy wrong.

Abby glanced over at Mr. Tressler. Could he help?

Snortle choke!

Mr. Tressler awoke.

"I didn't mean to startle you," Abby said.

Slowly, he reached for his cane. He pushed himself up a bit.

"Are you okay?" Abby asked, getting up.

"Just a bit dazed," he admitted. "But now that you're here, I'm fine. Sit down, missy." He patted the chair next to him.

Abby smiled. Mr. Tressler had a charming way about him. He could turn problems into pudding—sometimes.

Abby didn't spring her questions on him right away. She sat in the patio chair and chatted with him.

They talked about the sunny summer day. They listened to the *chirp-chirp-chirping* of the robins. And they laughed together.

Soon, it was time for lunch.

Time had passed so quickly. Abby hadn't asked Mr. Tressler anything. Not one word about the fighting in the cul-de-sac.

"Abby!" her mother called from the porch.

Abby could see Shawn and Jimmy running toward her house. "Well, I better go," she said.

"That's a girl." Mr. Tressler nodded. "Never keep your mother waiting."

She started to say something else. But she spotted Dunkum chasing Stacy. More trouble!

Stacy was carrying long black strands of yarn in her hand. Dunkum ran after her wearing a stovepipe hat. Dee Dee was right behind them—yelling!

"What's *this* about?" Abby muttered.

Mr. Tressler leaned forward. "Dear me—trouble in the cul-de-sac?"

Abby shook her head. "This whole mailbox thing is a mistake!" She hurried down the steps and across the street.

Stacy sprinted across her lawn and into her house.

Dunkum didn't let that stop him. He ran right up Stacy's steps. He began to pound on the door!

Dee Dee grabbed Abby's arm and pulled on her. "Make them give me back my mailbox stuff!"

"Is that Abe Lincoln's beard and top hat?" Abby asked.

Dee Dee nodded. "Stacy and Dunkum are fighting. They're fighting over who's gonna help me."

Abby felt helpless. What could she do?

Nine

Abby stood there watching.

She wanted to drag Dunkum down off Stacy's steps. She wanted to shake him and tell him to stop.

Poor Dee Dee, she thought. *This is all my fault.*

"Can't you do something?" Dee Dee pleaded.

"I'm sorry," Abby said. "Not now. I have to go in for lunch." She headed across the yard.

"Abby!" yelled Dee Dee.

"Go ring Stacy's doorbell," Abby called. "Maybe she'll talk to *you*." Sadly, she headed home.

■■■

Abby could hardly eat.

Shawn and Jimmy sat across from each other at the table. They scowled.

Carly whined and refused to look at Abby. All through lunch.

Mother looked first at Abby, then the others. "What's going on with the four of you?"

Abby spoke up. "Everything's horrible. We're having a mailbox-decorating contest. But nothing's working out."

Carly smirked. "*My* mailbox is ready."

Shawn shook his head. "We must make mailbox together. Four Hunter kids . . . together."

"Remember our meeting?" Abby said. "Remember what Eric said about working together? We're a family."

Carly poked out her bottom lip. "I wish we weren't!"

Mother's eyebrows bounced up. "Carly Anne Hunter!"

"Well, it's true!" Carly wailed. And she got up and stomped off.

Mrs. Hunter excused herself and left the table.

Shawn's eyes got big. Jimmy's too.

And Abby felt like a jitterbug.

Ten

It was the day before the Fourth.

And the day before Mailbox Mania.

Abby sat under a tree in the front yard. She stared at their mailbox. It was all red and white now. Like a flag.

All the Hunter kids had decorated the mailbox. Mother's talk with Carly had changed everything!

Abby was glad.

Next door, Stacy's mailbox was on display, too. It was blue, with perfect white and red stars. And an American flag for the mailbox flag!

Abby tried not to look at Stacy's beautiful mailbox. But her eyes weren't helping.

Then Shawn and Jimmy brought the dog

over. Snow White was panting. "She is very hot," Shawn said.

Jimmy just stood there. His eyes were blank.

Abby nodded. "I'm hot, too. But not from the heat." She shot a mean look at Jimmy.

"You are mad, yes?" Shawn said.

"Jimmy doesn't like our mailbox," Abby said. "I thought the fighting was over!"

When Jimmy heard that, he ran across the street. He sat on Eric's lawn and stared at them.

Abby wished she were an only child. Like Stacy and Eric. And all the other Cul-de-Sac Kids.

■■■

When the mail came, Abby ran to get it. She reached for the letters. But there was something else inside.

A present. With a bright red bow.

"What's this?" she said.

Jimmy dashed over for a look. "Let me see." He peered inside.

"It's a present." Abby took it out.

Jimmy stood on tiptoes. "Is present for me?"

Abby looked at the card. "It's for you . . . and Carly, Shawn, and me."

Jimmy jumped up and down. "Yippee!"

"Quick, let's find the others," Abby said.

"Open it!" Jimmy shouted.

Abby dashed into the house. "Carly!" she called. "There's a present for all of us in the mail!"

That brought her running.

Soon, the four of them were tearing off the paper. Abby opened the lid. Shawn, Jimmy, and Carly leaned closer.

Abby held up the gift. "It's a puzzle piece."

"With words on it," Carly said.

Jimmy's face wrinkled up. "That not present."

Abby stared at the puzzle piece. "I can't see all the words. Something's missing."

Shawn and Carly each took a turn looking at the puzzle piece. "Who sent us this?" Carly asked.

"I don't know," Abby said. "It's a mystery."

Shawn laughed. "A mystery in the mailbox!"

Just then, the doorbell rang.

Carly ran to get it.

It was Stacy. "Look what I got in the mail." She held up a puzzle piece.

Abby studied it. "You got one, too?"

The doorbell rang again.

It was Eric and Jason this time.

"Someone put puzzle pieces in our mail-boxes," Eric said.

Jason danced around when he saw Abby's piece. And Stacy's. "Hey! Maybe they fit to-gether!"

The kids knelt down on the floor. Stacy and Eric moved their pieces around. They didn't fit Jason's piece. So they switched.

"Wait . . ." Abby laughed as Stacy's piece snapped into hers. "This is double dabble good!"

Carly giggled. "Let's see if Dunkum and Dee Dee got puzzles, too."

"Good idea," the kids said. They picked up their puzzle pieces and dashed out the front door.

Eleven

The Cul-de-Sac Kids met Dunkum coming up the street. He was waving his present in the air.

Right there on the sidewalk, they tried to put the puzzle together.

"Look at that!" Abby said. "We're missing one piece."

Shawn tried to read the words. "It say something about us—the Cul-de-Sac Kids!"

The kids leaned over the puzzle. Their heads almost touched.

"You're right," Abby said. She smiled at Carly. "Why don't you go find Dee Dee?"

Carly leaped up. "Okay!" She ran down the street to Dee Dee's house.

Whoosh! Dee Dee flew out of her house. She checked her mailbox.

Abby and the others watched.

Dee Dee smiled when she spotted the present.

Carly was standing close by. She whispered in Dee Dee's ear and pointed to the other Cul-de-Sac Kids.

Dee Dee let out a "Yahoo!" She scurried down Blossom Hill Lane. Toward them.

Abby and the rest of the kids circled around her.

Dee Dee looked at the unfinished puzzle and set her piece down. Right in the middle.

It fit!

"*Now* we can read it," said Abby.

The kids read out loud. "The Cul-de-Sac Kids stick together."

They looked at one another. *Really* looked.

Abby smiled and gave Carly a hug. Then Jimmy came over and hugged Abby.

Soon, everyone was hugging.

Except Jason. He was dancing! "We stick . . . stick . . . stick together," he sang.

"*Now* we do!" Abby said.

The kids cheered.

"Who gave us these puzzle presents?" Dunkum asked.

"I don't know," Dee Dee said.

"Me neither," Carly said. The two girls giggled.

Abby called a meeting right there on the spot. "The meeting will now come to order," she said. "Any old business?"

The kids grinned. "Forget the old stuff," they shouted.

Eric raised his hand. "We have a mystery to solve."

Stacy nodded. "We sure do!"

Abby called for a vote.

Nine hands flew up.

It was agreed—the Cul-de-Sac Kids would play detectives.

"What about Mailbox Mania?" Dee Dee asked. "Aren't we having a contest?"

"That's tomorrow," Carly told her. "*Today* we have something else to do!"

Abby gathered up the puzzle pieces and stuck them in her pocket. She fell in step with Stacy and Eric. The others were close behind.

They were all off to solve a mystery.

Twelve

W here do we start?" Jason asked.

Abby had an idea. "Let's talk to Mr. Pete, the postman. He might be up the street."

"Let's ride bikes and catch him!" Dunkum suggested.

The kids went home to get their bikes.

Mr. Pete was three streets up. He looked surprised when nine kids on nine bikes called and waved him down.

When he stopped, Dunkum and Abby rode up to the mail truck.

"We need your help," Abby said.

"Something wrong?" he asked.

She explained about the presents.

"Why yes, I delivered them today," said Mr. Pete.

Dunkum frowned. "But there weren't any stamps on them."

Mr. Pete nodded. "I noticed that, too."

Abby watched his eyes. Something wasn't quite right. She watched his mouth. Mr. Pete was almost smiling.

"How can presents show up in mailboxes like that?" Abby asked.

Mr. Pete shook his head. "It's the strangest thing."

"Come on," Eric piped up. "*You* know how the post office works."

"I certainly do." Mr. Pete glanced at his watch. "And the U.S. Post Office wants the mail delivered on time. So if you'll excuse me . . ." And off he went.

Dunkum scratched his head. "I think he knows something."

"Maybe we should follow him," Jason said.

"We better stick close to home," Stacy said.

"We better stick together," Abby said, grinning.

They zoomed down the hill toward their

cul-de-sac. And stopped in front of Dunkum's house.

"I'm starved," Jason said. "Let's have a picnic."

"Where?" Stacy asked.

"Mr. Tressler has the biggest yard," Abby said. "Besides, we haven't visited him much. Not all of us together."

"Good idea," Shawn said.

"Who wants to pack a lunch for Mr. Tressler?" Abby asked.

Nine hands went up. Abby voted, too.

"Let's everyone bring something!" Dee Dee said.

And they did.

■■■

Mr. Tressler seemed to enjoy the company. He nodded and smiled when Abby sat next to him—beside the comfortable lawn chair.

After dessert, the kids showed him the puzzle pieces. Jason pushed through the circle and put the puzzle together. "Look at that," he bragged. "Five seconds flat!"

"Any second grader can do that," Dee Dee teased.

Jason took the puzzle apart. He passed the pieces to Dee Dee. "OK, you'll be in second grade next year. Let's see how fast you are."

The kids watched her put the puzzle together. "The Cul-de-Sac Kids stick together," they chanted when it was done.

Mr. Tressler leaned forward to look. "What a fine puzzle."

"Looks homemade," Abby said. "Don't you think so?"

Jason popped up. "We want to find out who sent the pieces to us."

Carly giggled. "The mailman acted funny."

"You should have seen him," Dunkum said. "He was in a big hurry."

"I think he's keeping a secret," Eric said.

Mr. Tressler listened. Then he said, "What sort of secret?"

"We don't know yet," Abby said.

Mr. Tressler rubbed his chin. "Looks to me like you've got yourselves a mystery."

Stacy looked at her watch. "We can't spend all day solving it. Tomorrow is Mailbox Mania!"

Mr. Tressler sat up straight. "And I get to

choose the best mailbox!" He tapped his cane on the ground.

Abby looked at Jimmy and Carly. She looked at Shawn. "I don't know about the rest of you, but—" She paused.

Dunkum smiled. "I think I know what Abby's going to say."

"So do I," Carly said.

Mr. Tressler's face burst into a grin. "You don't need a judge? Is that it, missy?"

Abby nodded. "Maybe we should just have fun with Mailbox Mania. Without the contest." She looked around. "Let's vote on it."

The kids agreed.

"OK," she said. "How many for a mailbox contest?"

No hands.

"How many want just for fun?"

Nine hands. No . . . ten. Jason raised two!

Eric pushed one of Jason's hands down. "Hey, no fair voting twice!"

Jason frowned and pushed his hand back up. "I can if I want!"

"Whoa, there." Mr. Tressler raised his hand. "I thought the Cul-de-Sac Kids stuck together."

He turned and winked at Abby.

"Why, Mr. Tressler?" she exclaimed. "Do you know something we don't?"

"Let's have a look at that puzzle." He grinned at Abby and the others. "Five seconds, you say?"

Jason counted the seconds.

Mr. Tressler's bony fingers flew.

"Three seconds!" Jason shouted. "Mr. Tressler put the puzzle together in only *three* seconds!"

The kids cheered.

"Mr. Tressler made it!" Jason said. "*He* made the puzzle!"

"Thank you, Mr. Tressler," Abby said. "Thank you very much!"

Mr. Tressler's eyes twinkled.

The mystery was solved.

BOOK 10

The Mudhole Mystery

For Emily,
who likes to make
muddy messes,
mostly in
Minnesota.

One

Splash, splish.

Big globs of mud mashed between Dunkum's fingers. He pressed his hands deep into the dirt. Digging for treasure was a great way to spend a Saturday.

Dunkum's real name was Edward Mifflin. His friends called him Dunkum. He was very tall. And the best basketball player around.

Basketball was the last thing on Dunkum's mind today. He was dreaming of gold and jewels. Maybe the pirate kind.

Today was May twenty-second. A special day. His grandma's holiday book called it Mysteries Are Marvelous Day.

Dunkum loved mysteries. Today was a

good day to dig for one. Gold or gems. Anything would do!

He really didn't know if there was treasure in the hole. But it didn't matter. He loved the ooshy-gooshy feel.

What a messy, mucky hole it was—a giant one. It was the biggest mudhole in the world. Well, in the cul-de-sac.

Suddenly, Dunkum's fingers touched something slimy. Out of the goop, he pulled a long, skinny worm.

"Maybe I should save this creepy creature for Stacy Henry. She hates worms."

"Says who?" someone called behind him.

Dunkum looked around.

Stacy was standing there, grinning.

Gulp.

"Oh, hi," he said. Dunkum tossed the worm back into the muddy brown pudding.

Burp! The mudhole belched right there in Mr. Tressler's backyard.

"You were talking to yourself, weren't you?" Stacy asked.

Dunkum didn't answer.

"I heard you." Stacy stared at him, then at the mudhole. "What a horrible mess."

Dunkum pulled out a mound of mud. "Care for a glob of pudding?"

Stacy shook her head. "I hate dirt. Messes too."

"No kidding," Dunkum whispered. He threw the mud back into the hole. *Splat!*

"Remember Pet Day?" Dunkum said. "Remember when Jason's bullfrog landed on your lap?"

Stacy twisted her blond hair. "So what?"

Dunkum continued. "You had to go wash the froggy feel off your hands. That's what." He laughed about it.

"It's not nice to dig up the past," Stacy said.

Dunkum stuck his hands back into the mud bubble. Deeper and deeper into the gloppy bog, he pushed.

He was up to his funny bones on both arms. No one tickled his funny bone and got away with it. But something was definitely thumping his left elbow. And it wasn't a tickle. It was a bumpity bump.

"Hey!" he hollered at the mudhole. "Quit that."

Stacy laughed at him. "Now who are you talking to?"

"The mudhole, that's who." Dunkum hit the ooshy-gooshy mud again.

There was definitely something there. Something big.

Dunkum's eyes grew wide. "Hey! Maybe I've found a mystery!" He shoved his hands in deeper.

Stacy stepped back. She sure didn't want to get her new outfit dirty. Or her sneakers. "What is it?" she asked.

Dunkum's eyes were slits as he grabbed something and pulled hard. "A mystery in a mudhole," he whispered.

He was thinking again of pirates and treasure.

What *was* in the mudhole?

Two

Dunkum stirred the mud around. He swirled and mixed it. He struggled against the hard lump.

"Maybe it's a dinosaur bone," he said.

"Cool!" Stacy said. "We could put it on display. Maybe start a museum."

Just then, the mudhole gobbled up Dunkum's arms.

Stacy yelled, "I can't see your elbows!"

Dunkum grunted and shoved. His face was down close to the mud. "The lump is too big. I need a shovel."

Click. Someone was opening Mr. Tressler's yard gate.

Dunkum looked up. There stood Jason

Birchall. He was carrying his bullfrog, Croaker.

"Who needs a shovel?" Jason asked.

Stacy spoke up. "Dunkum thinks he found a dinosaur bone."

Jason pushed up his glasses. "Croaker doesn't see any dinosaur bones. Do you, old buddy?"

Stacy giggled. "Since when do frogs understand English?"

"Croaker does," Jason said. He knelt beside Dunkum in the mud. "Where's the bone? Is it a T-Rex T-bone?"

Dunkum shook his head. "I don't know yet. But whatever it is, it's big. Very big."

Stacy stared into the sloppy mudhole. "Icksville," she said.

Suddenly, Dunkum saw a flash of gold. His eyes bugged out. "Hey, did you see that?"

Jason spotted it, too. "It's definitely gold!"

Stacy stepped closer. Her eyes were as round as quarters.

"Here, hold my frog," Jason said to Stacy.

Stacy held up her hands. "No . . . uh, not today."

"He's *not* slimy, and he doesn't bite," Jason joked.

"I know that," Stacy said.

"Here, just take him. You'll be fine," Jason said. And he handed Croaker to Stacy.

Stacy took the bullfrog. She held him far away from her. Croaker's skin felt smooth and thin, like a balloon filled with air. She felt his lungs moving. In and out. Out and in.

Stacy shivered. She thought she was going to drop Croaker. His body felt so weird.

Then she glanced at the muddy mess. The mudhole.

Dunkum was covered with muck. Jason dived into the mudhole. Hands first.

Stacy looked at the bullfrog. Croaker's round eyes blinked back at her.

She smiled. "Frog-sitting is much better than mess making!"

The mudhole squelched and blubbered.

Out of the spurting muddy custard came something shiny. It really *was* gold.

"Hey, we're rich!" Jason shouted.

"We aren't rich," Dunkum said. "Our treasure is stuck in the mud."

Stacy looked at the shiny gold. "Looks like a lock."

Dunkum nodded. "It's connected to something much bigger. But I don't know what."

Stacy inched closer for a better look.

Croaker blinked his froggy eyes. His lungs breathed in and out.

Dunkum and Jason kept working. They pulled and tugged. They grunted and groaned.

"It's in there for keeps," Dunkum said. "I can't lug it out."

Jason began scooping handfuls of mud out of the hole.

When more mud was removed, the boys tried again. They jerked and yanked. They fussed and yelped.

But the mudhole wouldn't let go.

Jason was tired. He stood up, all muddy.

"Well, *I'm* not quitting," Dunkum announced.

Stacy headed for the gate. "I'll get the rest of the Cul-de-Sac Kids. Maybe *all* of us can pull out the mystery."

"Hurry!" Dunkum said, looking at the mudhole. "I think our gold is sinking!"

Three

Something huge was in the mudhole!
Dunkum wondered, *Could it be a mummy?*

He went back to digging.

After several minutes, Jason said, "It's no use. We can't get it out." And he let go again.

"Please don't quit," Dunkum pleaded. "My fingers are slipping. I need your help."

Jason leaped back toward the hole. He grabbed on to the giant lump. He held it with all his might.

"You're pushing it down!" shouted Dunkum.

Jason let go and crawled away. His face was caked with mud. Even his nose. He tried to brush it off. It smeared.

"Just pretend it's beef gravy," Dunkum laughed.

Jason pulled a handkerchief out of his pocket. He blew his nose. Now the handkerchief was a yucky brown.

"Gross," Dunkum said.

Jason licked his muddy fingers. "Yummy chocolate pudding," he joked. Then he spit out the dirt.

Dunkum glared at him. "Excuse me," he said. He was still hanging on to the muddy lump. "Do you have a shovel?"

"I'll go home and check," Jason said. He stood up. Thick mud stuck to his arms and legs. It was in his hair. Splashes of mud spotted his glasses.

Dunkum scolded. "Wait till your mom sees you!"

"I'll be right back," Jason called. He ran down the street.

Dunkum was determined. He wanted the lumpy bump out of the mudhole. The lump with the gleaming *gold* object!

For a moment, he relaxed his grip and stood up. It felt good to stretch his legs. But he wasn't happy. He frowned at the mudhole.

Dunkum knew one thing for sure: He wasn't going home till the mudhole let go!

■■■

Soon, the rest of the Cul-de-Sac Kids showed up.

Abby Hunter took one look at Dunkum. She shook her head. "Yuck, what a mess," she said.

"I told you it was icksville," Stacy said. She was still holding Croaker.

Abby and her little sister, Carly, stared at Dunkum. And at the mudhole.

"Does Mr. Tressler know you're digging in his yard?" Carly asked.

Dunkum turned around. He glanced at Mr. Tressler's back porch. "I've been digging here for years."

"Well, you ought to ask first," Carly said. Her blond curls danced.

"Don't be bossy," Abby scolded.

Shawn and Jimmy Hunter ran over to the mudhole.

"We help, yes?" Shawn said. He and Jimmy were still learning English. It was hard because they were born in Korea. They were Abby and Carly's adopted brothers.

Dunkum shook his head. "I could use some serious help. Anyone have a rope?"

"I not," Jimmy Hunter said.

Abby had an idea. "Let's make a human chain."

Eric Hagel chuckled. "Where's my camera?" The kids laughed.

Stacy looked around. "Where'd Jason go?"

"I'm coming!" he shouted. Jason was dragging a big shovel.

"All right!" Dunkum said. "Now maybe we can solve the mudhole mystery."

Four

Jason came running. He plopped the shovel down and pushed it into the mudhole.

Dunkum and Shawn clawed at the dirt with their hands. Eric and Jimmy pushed piles of mud away.

Dee Dee Winters watched as she held her cat. "Mister Whiskers wants to help, too," she said.

Suddenly, Dee Dee's cat laid eyes on Croaker. Mister Whiskers meowed and spit at the bullfrog.

"Aw, kitty, that's not nice," Dee Dee scolded.

Stacy hid Croaker under her jacket. "I guess cats and frogs don't mix," she said.

Dee Dee finally got her cat settled down. She stood beside Abby and Carly and watched

the boys dig. They were making an even bigger mess.

"Wow! Look at that!" Carly shouted.

Something big was coming out of the mud.
It was half in, half out. The mystery lump
was a square box.

"What can it be?" Abby said.

"We're gonna find out!" Jason hollered.

Dunkum and Jason were still kneeling in
the mudhole.

"It's almost out," Jason said.

"Let's pull the box out together," Dunkum
suggested.

Abby and Carly grabbed Dunkum's arms.

"I'm ready!" Carly shouted.

"Me too," Abby said, grinning.

Stacy and Dee Dee decided not to help.
They didn't want to get dirty. Besides, they
were trying to end a frog and cat war.

Mister Whiskers kept hissing at Croaker.

Dee Dee tried to make her cat behave. She
even promised him a new litter box. "Just
be nice, OK?"

Mister Whiskers played dumb.

"I'll make it a *blue* litter box," Dee Dee
said. "How's that?"

Meow.

Mister Whiskers was spoiled rotten.

"Showtime!" Dunkum called to his friends.

Eric held on to Dunkum's belt loops.

Shawn gripped Jason's T-shirt.

Little Jimmy latched on to Shawn's back pocket.

"On the count of three, we'll lift it out," Dunkum said.

Together, the boys hollered, "One . . . two . . . three!"

Five

The boys pushed and pulled. They forced and twisted.

With a mighty heave, the mudhole sneezed. *Ah-ah-ahrga-choo!*

Out flew a square box.

The kids fell backward. Then they saw the old chest.

"Wow!" said Abby. She crept close to the muddy chest. "There's a gold latch and lock on it."

"That's the gold we saw," Dunkum said. He was a little disappointed because he was hoping for the real thing.

Jason rubbed his muddy hands together. "Could it be a secret treasure?"

"Let's have a look," Dunkum said.

Stacy's eyes grew big. "Can't you clean it off first?"

"Who cares about a little dirt?" Jason said. He hopped around like a rabbit.

Dunkum smeared his arm across the top of the box. "There. Now it's not so bad."

Carly shook her head. "It's still yucky."

"Maybe for you," Jason said. "Not for me." And he stood in the mud beside Dunkum, Eric, Shawn, and Jimmy.

Dunkum looked at his friends. All the Cul-de-Sac Kids were gathered around. *They all want to open it*, he thought.

"I'll open the lid," Jason said. He grabbed hold of the chest before Dunkum could stop him.

"It's so-o exciting," Stacy said.

Dunkum felt his stomach flip-flop. This was *his* chest. How dare Jason just barge in like this!

Jason bent over the chest. "Is everyone dying to see what's inside?" he asked.

Dunkum could see how excited Jason was. He didn't want to be a poor sport. "Whenever you're ready," Dunkum said.

Shawn chuckled. "One . . . two . . . three!" he counted.

Jason tried to pry the chest open. His face turned two shades of pink. "Whew! It must be locked."

"Let me try," Eric said. He showed off his muscles.

The kids laughed.

Shawn counted to three again.

Eric leaned down and pulled. "Oof!"

But the lid wouldn't move.

Stacy pointed to the gold latch. "Look! It *has* to be locked."

The boys took turns observing the problem.

Dunkum jiggled the latch.

Jason poked at it.

Eric knocked with his fist.

Shawn studied the lock.

Jimmy talked Korean to it.

The lock was definitely doing its job.

"I wonder where the key might be," Stacy said.

"There's got to be a key," Dunkum added.

Eric shook the lock again. "Why would someone bury a locked chest?"

Dunkum frowned. "I wish I knew."

Six

W e need a plan," Dunkum said.

Abby spoke up. "Let's have a meeting."

Jason jigged around. "Somebody call the meeting to order!" he announced.

"Sit down and we will," Dunkum said.

Jason plopped down on top of the muddy chest.

"Eew!" the girls shrieked.

Jason just sat there, grinning. "What's the problem?" he asked. "Mud washes off. Right?"

Stacy shook her head. "I really don't know about you, Jason Birchall."

Dunkum whistled. "OK, we need to think of a plan. A way to open the chest."

"Hey, you forgot to call the meeting to order," Eric said.

"Abby's the club president," said Dee Dee. "Let her do it."

Abby tossed her a smile. "The meeting will come to order. Any old business?"

"Yeah," said Jason. He stuck his foot up. "I've got super muddy sneakers. Anybody worried?"

Carly and Dee Dee giggled.

"Well, at least *The Stinky Sneakers Mystery* is solved!" said Eric.

"No comment," Jason said.

"Now for the new business," Abby said. "Dunkum says we need a plan. Any ideas?"

"We should pick the lock," Carly said. "Try a toothpick or something."

"Why didn't *I* think of that?" Dunkum said.

Before anyone could say "mudhole mystery," Dunkum had dashed out the gate.

"That was quick," Dee Dee said.

And it was.

In a flash, Dunkum was back with a box of toothpicks. He tried to spring the lock. One toothpick after another snapped in half.

"The problem is the mud," Dunkum said. "It's all caked up in there."

"Let me try," Stacy said. She handed Croaker to Jason. "I'm a fixer-upper."

Abby agreed. She and Stacy were best friends. Stacy had come to her rescue many times. "Stacy has a steady hand," said Abby. "Maybe *she* can unlock the mystery chest."

The kids leaned in closer. They watched as Stacy tried the toothpick trick.

After three tries, Stacy shook her head. "I think we need a different plan."

Jason said, "Let's try a hammer."

"Smash the lock?" Abby said. "Is that a good idea?"

"We want the silly thing unlocked, don't we?" Eric asked.

"Eric's right," Jason piped up.

"Whoa," said Dunkum. "Maybe we should vote on it."

Abby called for the vote. "How many want to use the hammer method?"

Everyone voted yes. Everyone except Dee Dee and Abby.

Jason was clapping. "Seven to two. We win!" Off he ran to his house. "Don't do anything without me," he called.

Abby went to the chest. She rubbed off

some more mud. "Hey, look at this," she said. "There's writing on it."

The kids pressed near the chest. "What does it say?" they asked.

"It's hard to see," Abby said. "I think we need some soap and water."

"I'll ask Mr. Tressler about his garden hose," Eric said. "Maybe we could use it."

Dunkum ran to Mr. Tressler's back door.

Soon, the man was outside, standing on his deck. "My, oh my. Did all of you come for a visit?" He cheerfully waved his cane at the kids.

The kids waved back.

Abby hurried across the lawn. "We hope you don't mind," she said. "Dunkum's found a mudhole he likes to dig in and—"

"There's a *hole* in my yard?" Mr. Tressler said. "Where?"

"Come, we'll show you." Abby led the old gentleman to the mudhole. Dunkum followed close behind. He was a bit worried now.

Mr. Tressler leaned on his cane and looked down at the mudhole. "Well, what do you know. . . ." His voice stopped.

Dunkum was even more worried. "I've been

digging here for the longest time. Before anyone lived here."

Mr. Tressler's eyes squinted. "Is that so?"

Dunkum thought, *Am I in trouble?*

Mr. Tressler saw the muddy chest. "Just
what do we have here?"

"It's something we found," Dunkum explained.

Mr. Tressler wasn't smiling. "Looks to me
like you *dug* it up. Dug it right out of my
yard."

"Uh . . . yes, sir, we did," Dunkum said. He
wanted to tell the old man about all the fun
they'd had. About the shiny gold lock. But
something made him stop. It was the frown
on Mr. Tressler's face.

"This is *my* property," Mr. Tressler said.
"You should have asked me."

Dunkum felt jittery.

"That's only good manners," Mr. Tressler
explained.

Dunkum sighed. "I'm sorry about the hole.
We should have talked to you first."

"It's too late for that," Mr. Tressler said.

Dunkum saw Jason running down the
street. He was waving a hammer.

Mr. Tressler turned around in time to see Jason. "What's that in his hand?" the man asked.

The kids stared at Dunkum.

Dunkum gulped. They were going to smash the lock on a chest. On something they'd found in a mudhole. Something that didn't belong to any of them.

Jason was out of breath. "I came as fast as I could."

Mr. Tressler turned and looked at Jason. "What's the hammer for, young man?"

Jason's eyes blinked. Fast.

Like Croaker's, thought Dunkum.

Jason looked first at Dunkum, then at Mr. Tressler. "I . . . uh . . . I . . ." Jason tried to speak.

This isn't Jason's fault, thought Dunkum. He felt sorry. Sorry and sad.

But what could Dunkum say?

Seven

Digging was *my* idea," Dunkum blurted. "Not Jason's."

Mr. Tressler rubbed his pointy chin. "I see."

"Dunkum's telling the truth," Abby said.

Mr. Tressler looked at each of the Cul-de-Sac Kids. "Exactly what is going on here?"

Dunkum took a deep breath. "I was playing in the mud," he began. "Something hard was in there. I wanted to get it out. Really bad."

Abby nodded. "That's when Stacy got all of us to come. We helped Dunkum pull out the old chest."

"Interesting," said Mr. Tressler. He tapped his cane on the ground. "Tell me more."

Abby stood beside him. "Something is written on it. Come look!"

Mr. Tressler hobbled over to the old chest. Abby showed him where the faint letters were printed. Right on top.

"We wanted to borrow your garden hose," Jason chimed in. "So Abby could read the words."

Mr. Tressler tried to brush off the drying mud. He peered down at the dim writing. "Yes, yes. I see what you mean." He turned around and ordered Jason to get the hose.

"Yes, sir!" Jason said. And off he ran to the house.

■■■

The garden hose cleaned things right up. It cleaned the kids' hands, too.

The Cul-de-Sac Kids took turns reading these words: *Time Capsule—Beware!*

Dunkum's heart was pounding. "We have to get the chest open." He remembered that he should ask. "Um, Mr. Tressler, is it OK with you?"

Dunkum saw a familiar twinkle in the man's eyes.

"Well now, you and your friends better get a move on," Mr. Tressler ordered.

"Yes!" Dunkum cheered.

"Double dabble good!" Abby shouted.

"Let's open the time capsule!" Jason hollered. He handed the hammer to Dunkum.

Dunkum raised the hammer high.

"Wait!" said Shawn. "We count first."

Dunkum knew what Shawn meant. "OK. You do the counting."

Shawn's dark eyes sparkled. "One . . . two . . . three!"

Carly and Jimmy covered their ears.

Ka-whack!

The hammer hit hard.

The lock popped.

"It's open!" Eric shouted. And he and the others pulled up the lid.

The kids crowded around. They stared into the chest.

"Wow, this is so cool," said Stacy.

"I've never seen a real time capsule," Dunkum said.

"What are the paper bags for?" Carly asked.

Jimmy leaned over and poked at the brown bags inside the chest.

Dunkum said, "Looks like someone wrapped up things in lunch bags."

Jimmy took a closer look. "I never see time capsule in Korea," he said. He reached down and pulled something out. "Open, yes?"

"First, Mr. Tressler should have a look," Dunkum said.

Jimmy held on to the squished paper bag.

Mr. Tressler leaned over and peeked, too. "What are we waiting for? Let's unwrap the loot!"

Dunkum didn't have to be told twice. "Go for it!" he said with a grin.

Eight

The Cul-de-Sac Kids reached into the chest. They pulled out packages of different sizes and shapes. Some long and some short. Some giant sized and some mini.

Abby had a suggestion. "Someone should be taking notes."

"Good idea," Eric said. "But who's gonna get the paper and a pencil?"

The kids looked at one another. No one seemed interested. Not with a time capsule right in front of their noses.

"Aw, forget that," Jason said. He stared at the package in his hands.

Some of the kids agreed. "Yeah, forget it," they said.

Abby frowned. "Don't tell me—we have to vote about this, too?"

"No!" Dunkum said. He was sick of voting. "Somebody start opening."

"I start," said Jimmy.

RIP! He tore the old paper bag.

Jimmy held up a cardboard tube. "Too hard to open," he said.

Mr. Tressler pulled out his pocketknife. "Here you are, young fella. This will help."

Dunkum helped Jimmy cut open the long tube.

"Hey, check this out," Dunkum said. He unrolled a piece of paper. When it was flattened, he held it up. "It's a note."

"Read it!" Jason said.

Dunkum scanned the page. "It says, 'If you find this time capsule, it belongs to you.'"

"Hey, that's us!" Dee Dee said.

It belongs to me, thought Dunkum.

"Keep reading," Abby said.

"OK." Dunkum continued. "'The objects in this time capsule will tell all about us.'"

"Us?" Stacy said. "Who is *us*?"

"Is the paper signed?" asked Eric.

Dunkum looked closely. "It's signed 'The Cul-de-Sac Club—CDSC.'"

"Wow," Jason said. "There must have been *other* kids living here—in the cul-de-sac!"

"Yeah, long before us," said Abby.

"Who were they?" asked Dee Dee.

"Where are they now?" said Dunkum.

Mr. Tressler waved his cane. "I have an idea," he said. "Why not open the rest of the packages? Maybe you'll find out."

"I'm next!" Jason said.

Everyone watched Jason pull out a tattered book. "Hey," he said. "It's a Sherlock Holmes mystery."

Dunkum's mouth dropped open. "You're kidding."

"Nope," said Jason. "See for yourself."

Dunkum looked at the book. "This is so weird."

"What's weird about an old book?" Abby asked.

Dunkum's face looked strange. Almost white. "I'll tell you what," he said. His voice was almost a whisper. "Today is May twenty-second."

"So?" Jason said.

"What's special about May twenty-second?" Stacy asked.

Dunkum took a deep breath. "Today is Mysteries Are Marvelous Day. It's to celebrate Sir Arthur Conan Doyle's birthday," he explained.

"Who's Sir Arthur . . . whatever the rest of his name is?" Carly asked. She flipped one of her curls.

Dunkum glanced at Mr. Tressler. "*You* know, don't you?" he asked the old gentleman.

Mr. Tressler nodded. "I certainly do. You see, when I was a boy, Sherlock Holmes was my hero. Sir Arthur Conan Doyle wrote my favorite books. He was born on this very day—back in 1859."

"Wow," Abby said. "No wonder Dunkum was freaked out."

"It's mighty strange, if I do say so myself," Mr. Tressler remarked.

Dunkum couldn't believe it. Here it was May twenty-second, and he'd found a time capsule. With a Sherlock Holmes book!

Some kid had lived around here long ago. He'd loved mysteries, too. Probably someone Dunkum's age.

Where was that kid now?

Nine

Stacy unwrapped another object. It was a word puzzle book. The answers were all filled in.

Next it was Abby's turn. Then Carly's.

Shawn and Eric came next. Last were Dee Dee and Dunkum.

The pile of items was growing. There was a dog collar and dish. And a Sunday school lesson.

A baseball glove, a ball, and a pack of gum. The glove was ratty. The gum was rock hard.

There were rock collections and pressed wild flowers. And dried-up gold aspen leaves.

A heavy box of green toy soldiers came next. An empty bird's nest, too.

Last of all, a tiny watch. Not gold, but pretty.

"Hey, look," Carly said. "It's the wind-up kind."

The girls studied it curiously.

"What are we gonna do with all this stuff?" Jason asked.

Abby started to make a neat stack. Stacy helped.

"I guess we should talk to *you*, Mr. Tressler," said Dunkum. "Do you mind if we keep these things?"

The old man shook his head. "Do as you wish." He leaned on his cane. "I believe it's time for my lunch." Mr. Tressler turned toward the house.

Dunkum called to him, "Thanks for everything!"

Mr. Tressler nodded without turning around.

"Happy Mysteries Are Marvelous Day!" shouted Dunkum.

That got a smile and a wave from Mr. Tressler. "The same to you," he said.

The kids put everything back inside the time capsule. Carefully, of course.

Dunkum looked at the square black chest. "How old is this thing, anyway?"

Jason didn't know.

But Eric had an idea. "Check the Sunday school lesson. There might be a date on it."

"Good thinking," Dunkum said. He found the old lesson sheet. On the bottom of the page was a date.

Abby peeked over Dunkum's shoulder. "Wow," she said. "This thing is twenty years old!"

Twenty years? thought Dunkum. *What a long time.*

"How old would the kids be now?" asked Carly.

"Figure it out," Eric said. "Pretend they were ten when they buried this."

"Easy," said Dee Dee. "Add ten years and twenty years. That's thirty!"

Dunkum's eyes lit up. "Hey, these kids are grown-ups now!"

"They . . . they are?" Jason sputtered.

"Yep," said Abby. "And they've probably forgotten all about the time capsule."

"Maybe not," said Dunkum.

"Hey, could we track down these kids . . . er, grown-ups?" Jason asked.

Eric shook his head. "Not in a million years."

Dunkum smiled. "Anything is possible."

"With God," Abby added.

Dunkum liked Abby's way of thinking best.

Ten

What are we gonna do with the time capsule?" Eric asked.

Carly shrugged. "Leave it here."

"Right here, where we found it," Dee Dee said.

We? thought Dunkum. *I found it first!*

"We'll take it to my house," Dunkum insisted.

Jason frowned. "No fair!"

"Why not?" Dunkum said. "I found it, didn't I?"

"But all of us helped pull it out," Jason said. He stood tall and stuck out his chest.

"Jason's right," Eric said. "Let's put the time capsule in Abby's backyard. She's the president of the Cul-de-Sac Kids."

Dunkum didn't want a fight. "OK. That makes sense," he said.

So Dunkum and Eric carried the time capsule down the street. Dee Dee carried Mister Whiskers. He was still hissing at Croaker.

Jason carried his frog a safe distance from the cat. The rest of the kids followed behind, like a parade. They arrived in the Hunters' backyard.

"Where should we put it?" Dunkum asked Abby.

"There," she pointed. "Under the tree."

Dunkum and Eric set the time capsule down near the swings. Beside the big tree.

"How's that?" Dunkum asked.

Abby's eyes shone. "Double dabble good."

The kids stood around. No one wanted to go home.

Dunkum walked toward the gate. "I'll be back after lunch," he called.

"Me too!" yelled Jason.

Carly asked Dee Dee to come back, too.

"Sure will," Dee Dee said.

That left Eric. He had to go to the dentist.

"I might come over later," he said. "If I feel good enough."

"What's wrong?" asked Abby. "Got a cavity?"

"Feels like it." Eric waved good-bye.

Dunkum said good-bye again. He was having a hard time leaving. He missed the time capsule already. *His* time capsule.

Everyone left, except the Hunter kids. They lived here. For a moment, Dunkum wished he lived here, too. Then he could see his time capsule any old time.

"OK, well, see you," Dunkum said.

"Alligator," Shawn said, grinning.

Abby told her brother how it went. "It's 'See you later, alligator. After a while, crocodile.' Get it?"

Shawn nodded. He laughed his high-pitched giggle.

Dunkum closed the backyard gate. He ran as fast as he could to his house next door. He thought about the time capsule. He wished it were at his house.

His dad was sitting on the front steps. He looked up from his newspaper. "Are you hungry?"

"Sure am," said Dunkum.

His dad put the newspaper away.

"Were you doing today's crossword puzzle?" asked Dunkum.

His dad nodded. "You know me well." He stuck the pencil above his ear. "Your mom's cooking hot dogs. Let's go eat."

Dunkum dashed up the steps.

"Whoa, just a minute." His dad had spotted the muddy clothes and shoes. "Where have *you* been?"

"Uh, just digging," Dunkum admitted.

"In mud? Better go wash up." His dad pointed to the garden hose.

Dunkum clumped to the side of the house. This was the second time today.

When he went inside for lunch, his mom frowned. "Why must you play in the mud?"

"Don't be hard on him, dear," Dunkum's dad said. "I did the same thing when I was a kid."

"I'll go change my clothes," Dunkum offered.

"Please don't track mud!" his mom called.

"I'll be careful," Dunkum said, tiptoeing downstairs.

He headed for the washroom. Dirty clothes were piled up. Saturday was not their wash-day.

Finally, Dunkum was cleaned up. He headed back to the kitchen. The table was set. The hot dogs and baked beans smelled great.

His mom asked about the muddy mess. But Dunkum didn't tell much about the mystery. Or the time capsule.

His parents were grown-ups. They'd forgotten what it was like to be a kid. Dunkum was sure of it!

Eleven

After lunch, Dunkum's dad returned to his newspaper. Word puzzles were one of his favorite hobbies.

Dunkum's favorites were shooting hoops and digging in the mud.

Today, basketball came in second. Dunkum had something else to do. He wanted to see the time capsule again.

And he had an idea. A great idea!

■■■

Dunkum hurried around to the Hunters' backyard.

The time capsule was still there.

Abby, Shawn, and Carly Hunter had just

finished lunch. They were outside looking in the chest. They pulled out many objects, looking and talking.

"We need to have another meeting," Dunkum said.

"Oh, hi, Dunkum." Abby turned around. "What's the meeting about?"

"About that." Dunkum pointed to the chest. "Let's make an exhibit."

"You mean like a museum or something?" Abby asked.

"Sure, why not?"

"Should we charge money?" Abby asked.

Dunkum walked over to the chest. "Yes. We could use the money for something special. For our club."

Jimmy was counting the rock collection in Korean.

Carly was trying on the pretty watch.

"This stuff is ancient history," said Dunkum. "It's at least twenty years old."

Abby nodded. "I see what you mean."

"When the rest of the kids come back, we'll decide," he said.

Abby grinned. "It's an excellent idea."

Dunkum leaned over and pulled out the

old Sherlock Holmes book. "I still can't believe this was in here."

Abby asked, "How did you know about Mysteries Are Marvelous Day?"

Dunkum told her about his grandma's holiday book. "It lists all kinds of special days."

"Like what?" Abby asked.

"Well, let's see." Dunkum thought for a second. "There's the birthday of basketball."

"You're kidding."

"Nope."

"When is it?" Abby asked.

"January fifteenth," Dunkum replied happily. "Back in the year 1892."

"Wow," she said. "What else?"

"Children's Day is May fifth," he said. "It's a national holiday in Korea and Japan. In honor of all children."

Shawn perked up his ears. "Yes, I know that. It is true."

"Your grandma's book sounds cool," Abby said.

"I'll ask her to bring it sometime," Dunkum said.

Just then, Jason came in the gate. Soon,

Stacy and Dee Dee were back. All the Cul-de-Sac Kids were present. Except Eric.

"Let's talk about your idea," Abby said to Dunkum.

"OK," he agreed. He began to tell the kids.

"I like museums," Stacy said. "This is a terrific idea."

Dee Dee and Carly thought the idea was silly.

"Who would pay to see all this junk?" Carly asked.

"You might be surprised," Dunkum said. "And it's not junk!"

Carly twirled her hair. "I'd rather ride bikes any day."

Dee Dee didn't say much. "If it makes money, that's good, I guess."

Jason wanted to be in charge of snack food. "Who wants to help me?"

"Wait a minute," Abby said. "We haven't voted yet."

"Let's wait for Eric," Dunkum said. "We don't want him to feel left out."

So they waited. And waited.

It was almost two o'clock. Eric still wasn't back.

"Oh well. We can vote tomorrow," Jason said.

"Tomorrow's Sunday," Abby said.

"OK, we'll vote after church," said Dunkum.

It was settled. They'd have a meeting and vote tomorrow.

Dunkum couldn't wait.

He thought about the vote. All through supper, he thought about it. And during his shower.

There were five boys and four girls. One of them might be a tie breaker.

Would his great idea fall flat?

Twelve

After church was dinner. Dunkum had to go home and eat. So did the other kids.

There was no time yet for a club meeting or the vote. Dunkum had to wait a little longer.

He poked at his dinner.

"Is something wrong?" Dunkum's mother asked.

He was silent.

"Dunkum?" his dad asked.

Finally, he looked up. "Have you ever had a great idea?"

"Lots of times," said his dad.

"When you were a kid?" Dunkum asked.

"Sure." His dad chuckled. "Why do you ask?"

Dunkum sighed. "Did you ever have to wait?"

His mother frowned. "What do you mean?"

"Did your friends have to decide if it was a good idea?"

Dunkum's dad nodded his head. "Sometimes, I guess."

"Then you must have had lots of friends," Dunkum said.

"You can say that again!"

"Well, I like discovering things by myself." Dunkum was thinking about his muddy discovery. "I'm not so sure if having lots of friends is good."

His parents stopped eating. They were staring at him.

Finally, his mother spoke. "You are the only child in our family. Is that why you feel this way?"

Dunkum nodded. "Maybe."

"Let me tell you something," his dad said. "A block full of friends can be good."

Dunkum listened.

"I grew up with three brothers and two sisters," his dad explained. "We were a kids' club all by ourselves."

Dunkum scratched his head. He couldn't imagine that many in the family.

"Six kids and two parents," his dad said. "Sometimes, Mom and Dad would pile us in the car. We liked to visit our uncle and aunt. They had three kids."

"That's a lot of kids all together!" Dunkum said.

His dad looked around the kitchen. "Can you imagine all of us eating here?"

Dunkum blinked his eyes. "You mean, right here? In Mom's kitchen?"

"Yep, this house belonged to Uncle Joe. We came here in the summers."

"A long time ago?" Dunkum asked.

His mother nodded. "Your father was eight the very first summer."

Dunkum laughed. It was hard to imagine. His dad had once been a kid. Long, long ago.

■ ■ ■

Eric showed up late for the meeting. "The dentist found *two* cavities yesterday," he explained.

"Are you better now?" Abby asked.

Eric nodded. "What did I miss?"

222

Carly piped up. "Oh, nothing much."

Dee Dee smiled a sly grin.

Dunkum tried to ignore Dee Dee and Carly. They were being a pain.

Today, he was eager. He explained his idea to *all* the kids this time.

When he was finished, Abby called for the vote. "How many want to make a display of the time capsule?" she asked.

Four hands shot up. Then one more.

"It's to raise money for our club," Jason said.

"No fair trying to get extra votes," Abby said.

Slowly, Eric and Stacy raised their hands.

But Dee Dee and Carly kept theirs down. Even without them, the vote had passed.

Abby cheered. So did Dunkum and Jason.

"We're gonna have the best time capsule exhibit ever!" Dunkum said.

■■■

Six days later, everything was ready.

The display was the hottest thing around!

Kids from Blossom Hill School came. So did cousins of the Cul-de-Sac Kids. Lots of parents came, too.

Stacy showed her mom the old watch. And the Sunday school lesson.

Shawn and Jimmy showed their parents the rock collection. Abby and Carly showed the crushed wild flowers.

Dunkum's parents seemed to enjoy themselves, too.

"What a wonderful idea, son," Dunkum's dad said.

"Thanks."

Suddenly, his dad stopped. Right in front of the giant word-puzzle book.

"What's wrong?" Dunkum asked.

His dad picked up the book and looked inside. He began to laugh. "This is *my* writing!"

"Yours?" Dunkum said. "How could that be?"

"Where did you find this stuff?" his dad asked.

"In Mr. Tressler's backyard."

Dunkum's father nodded his head, laughing. "Well, that makes sense."

Dunkum was confused. "Are you saying *you* buried the time capsule?"

"My brothers and cousins buried it. And so

did I." He grinned at Dunkum. "It was one of my great ideas."

Dunkum couldn't wait to tell his friends. He ran around the exhibit telling them. Mr. Tressler, too.

"What about the Sherlock Holmes book?" Mr. Tressler asked. "Did it belong to your father?"

"I'll ask," Dunkum said.

He found his dad counting the rock collection. Jimmy was counting, too. In Korean.

"What other stuff is yours?" Dunkum asked his dad.

"The crossword puzzle book and this." He pointed to the colorful rocks.

"What about the rest?" Dunkum asked.

His dad had to think. "The baseball glove was Uncle Joe's. He never knew what happened to it. The rest of the stuff belonged to my cousins and brothers."

"Not your sisters?" Dunkum asked.

"You know how some girls are about a great idea," he said. "Especially a muddy one."

Dunkum understood.

He glanced at Dee Dee and Carly across

the yard. They'd voted against him. Now they were helping Jason at the snack table.

Dunkum thought, *I'll invite them to make mud pies tomorrow.*

And that's what he did.

BOOK 11

Fiddlesticks

For Michael,
a soccer-lovin' fan
who eagerly awaits
the new books
in this series.

One

Shawn Hunter tuned his violin.

"Ready to practice?" his American sister asked.

"Almost." Shawn tucked the violin under his chin. He smiled at Abby. "Now ready."

Abby held the music. "High enough?"

"Very good," Shawn said. It came out like *velly* good.

Shawn was still learning to speak English. His first language was Korean. Abby's parents had adopted him and his little brother, Jimmy.

It was hard to get used to a new country. And a new school. But music lessons weren't new. Shawn, whose Korean name

was Li Sung Jin, loved music. Violin music most of all.

"I start now," Shawn said.

He drew the bow across the strings. A soaring melody filled the living room.

Abby tapped her toe to the music.

Suddenly, Shawn stopped playing.

"What's wrong?" asked Abby.

"Something missing," Shawn said.

He set his violin and bow on the sofa. He hurried down the hall to his bedroom.

Soon, he returned with his soccer ball.

"What's *that* for?" Abby asked.

"Ball help balance me," Shawn said.

He picked up his violin and bow. He set his right foot on top of the soccer ball. "That better."

Abby giggled.

Shawn began to play again.

He practiced major scales. Next, he reviewed two old songs. Then he worked on two new ones.

Over and over he practiced. Shawn loved playing his violin. As much as he loved playing soccer.

Shawn liked to dribble and punt. Sometimes

he practiced in his big backyard. Mostly when no one was watching.

Practicing in secret wasn't easy. But Shawn was determined to play with the Blossom Hill Blitzers. The team was named for Shawn's school. He wasn't sure what Blitzers meant. But it sounded good. Fast too.

◼◼◼

When Shawn finished practicing his violin, Abby clapped. "You sound double dabble good!" she said.

"Thank you." Shawn gave a stiff bow.

Woof!

Abby looked at their dog, Snow White. "What's the matter with you?" she asked the floppy-eared Shih Tzu.

Shawn laughed his high-pitched laugh. "Snow White not like violin music."

"Bad dog," Abby scolded. She went over and tickled her paws. Snow White was lying on her back. All four legs were sticking up. "Shawn makes nice music," she told the dog. "You don't have to play dead."

Shawn was still laughing. "Snow White need music lesson. She not understand."

"You're right," Abby said. She put the music away.

Shawn stopped laughing. Now he spoke softly. "Some *people* not understand, too."

"What?" Abby asked.

"Not important," Shawn muttered into his violin case.

Abby insisted. "What did you say?"

Shawn was silent.

He put his violin away. *Snap!* The lid clicked shut.

Abby sat on the floor and touched Shawn's arm. "Something's bugging you," she said. "You can't fool me."

Shawn sat beside her. "Abby good sister and *chingu*."

"Friends talk to each other," Abby said.

Shawn sighed. His dark almond-shaped eyes grew serious. He pushed his hand through his black hair.

"America hard place for Korean kid with violin," he admitted. "I not fit in."

"It takes time to get used to a new culture. But don't give up," Abby pleaded. She looked at him. "Are kids at school making fun of you?"

Shawn nodded sadly. "They have nickname for me."

Abby frowned. "What are they calling you?"

Shawn's eyes popped open. "Abby mad?"

"Yes, I'm mad!" She stood up. "What's the nickname?"

"They say make-fun name," he said. "They say, 'Fiddlesticks.' Because I skinny and . . . and small. And play violin. Boys not play violin in United States?"

"Of course they do," Abby said. She puffed air through her lips. "Who's calling you Fiddlesticks?"

"Kids who not like me," Shawn said.

Abby nodded. "I figured that, but who?"

"I not say." Shawn got up and walked toward the kitchen.

"Hey, come back!" Abby called.

But Shawn didn't answer. He couldn't.

There was a big lump in his throat.

TWO

The next day was Friday, March first.

Miss Hershey made an announcement to the class. "Today is the beginning of Music in Our Schools Month."

Shawn grinned. "Very good," he whispered.

Abby smiled at him across the row.

Shawn thought, *Music month great idea.*

Miss Hershey talked about composers. Famous ones. "The three B's," she called them. Bach, Beethoven, and Brahms.

She wrote on the chalkboard: *Bach has a birthday this month.*

"Who knows when this composer was born?" the teacher asked.

Shawn sat up straight. "I do!" he said. "1685, very long time."

Miss Hershey smiled. "Thank you, Shawn. That's correct. March 21, 1685. A long time ago, indeed." She wrote the date on the board.

While her back was turned, some kids made faces at Shawn. "Fiddlesticks," they said.

Abby heard.

So did Miss Hershey. "No talking, please!"

Shawn slumped in his seat. He couldn't help being small and thin.

He stared at Miss Hershey's desk. There was a suggestion box at one end. Miss Hershey emptied the box every Thursday. She read the suggestions to the class, and they discussed each one.

I write suggestion for box, thought Shawn. *I tell teacher about make-fun kids.*

Miss Hershey walked to her desk. "Class, please open to page 57 in your language arts notebook," she said. "We will work till recess."

Shawn looked in his desk. He found a notebook and pencil. He began to write his name on the work page.

"Ps-st—Fiddlesticks!" someone whispered. It was Ronny Kitch, the boy behind him.

"Hey, fiddle sticks boy," Ronny whispered again.

Shawn refused to turn around.

Ronny tapped Shawn's shoulder. "What page are we supposed to do?" he asked.

Slowly, Shawn turned. He was going to be nice. He was going to give Ronny the page number.

But now Ronny was making his eyes slant. He was pulling at his eyes on purpose. Making fun of Shawn. "Only a sissy plays a fiddle," Ronny hissed through his teeth.

In a flash, Shawn turned back around. He was *not* a sissy!

Instead of starting on the assignment, Shawn pulled out a fresh piece of paper. He glanced at Miss Hershey's suggestion box.

He wrote:

I not like to tattle. Students call me Fiddlesticks. Because I short, skinny person. Because I come from Korea and play violin.

Shawn read what he'd written. Then he picked up his pencil again.

I make suggestion for box. Can teacher make name stop? I thank you very much.

> *Respect to you,*
> *Shawn Hunter—*
> *Li Sung Jin*

Shawn folded the note and pushed it into his jeans. Before recess, he would visit the suggestion box.

"Hey, Fiddlesticks," Ronny said in his ear. "What do you think you're doing?"

Shawn froze.

Had Ronny seen the note?

Three

Ronny Kitch raised his hand. He waved it high.

"Yes, Ronny?" Miss Hershey said.

"I need to speak to you," he said.

Miss Hershey called him to her desk. They were whispering. Ronny shook his head. Then he turned and pointed to Shawn.

Miss Hershey's eyebrows flew up. "Shawn Hunter?" she said.

Quickly, Shawn stood up and bowed.

The kids snickered.

But Miss Hershey was kind. "In the United States, we don't bow when someone speaks to us," she explained. "Do you understand?"

Shawn nodded. He almost forgot and started to bow again.

"Will you please see me at morning break?" the teacher asked.

Shawn nodded again. "I come see you."

He sat down, worried. What had Ronny just told Miss Hershey?

Shawn thought and thought. He *had* been fooling around, not doing his work. Was Miss Hershey going to talk to him about *that*?

Ronny marched down the row of desks. He bumped against Shawn on the way back to his seat. He shoved him hard on purpose.

Miss Hershey was too busy to notice.

Shawn didn't like being pushed around. But he was a peanut next to Ronny. His arm muscles were like three jelly beans. His legs were like toothpicks.

Or . . .

Shawn swallowed the lump in his throat.

He looked down at his legs. They looked like violin bows. Like fiddle sticks.

No wonder the kids called him that!

Shawn sighed. He hoped Ronny wouldn't pick a fight. Even if Shawn wanted to fight, he couldn't beat him. Ronny was tough. He was mean.

Determined not to slouch, Shawn picked

up his pencil. He read the assignment and began to fill in the answers.

Abby glanced over at him. Her lips formed these words: *Are you OK?*

Shawn rubbed his nose. He formed these words back: *I OK.*

But he wasn't. Not really.

Abby turned her head and went back to work.

So did Shawn.

When he was finished, he took out a book about soccer. Miss Hershey wanted everyone to keep a library book handy. She called it free reading—when you finished work early.

Shawn liked books. English was still new to him, but he was a good reader. And smart. He wished he could talk better. Faster too.

The soccer book was exciting. From the time he'd learned to walk, Shawn liked to kick a ball around.

And two weeks from now, Shawn wanted to try out for the Blitzers. But he wanted to watch the boys practice *today*.

Then he remembered. His violin lesson was after school. What could he do?

Shawn stared at the pictures in the soccer

book. He thought about Ronny. Would *he* be
at soccer practice?

Shawn stopped thinking and started reading. The soccer book was wonderful. He
couldn't stop reading.

Soon, ideas were bouncing in his head.
Maybe he could watch practice after violin
lesson. Maybe he wouldn't be too late getting home.

He wished he could practice out on the
soccer field. He was tired of practicing in secret. The backyard was OK. But the gigantic
soccer field—that would be terrific!

Kids could dribble, punt, and kick on a
field like that. They could guard and do team
plays. Soccer drills—things that made a
great player.

Eric Hagel and Jason Birchall were good
players, too. They were two of Shawn's best
friends. Eric and Jason lived on his street, a
cul-de-sac. It was called Blossom Hill Lane,
close to Blossom Hill School.

Eric, Jason, and Shawn belonged to the
Cul-de-Sac Kids. Nine kids on one street.
Each one was Shawn's *chingu*—friend!

He was glad for friends. Very glad.

Then he remembered rotten Ronny Kitch.

He not chingu, Shawn thought.

Shawn closed the soccer book. He felt scared thinking about Ronny. *I forget about soccer team*, he thought. *I not try out*.

The bell rang for morning break.

Time to see Miss Hershey.

Shawn stood up. Slowly, he went to the front of the classroom.

"You see me, yes?" he asked.

"Let's talk," Miss Hershey said. "Have a seat."

Just then, Ronny ran outside for break. Shawn could hear him laugh. It was a loud laugh. A roaring laugh.

Shawn sat near Miss Hershey's desk.

She looked him in the eyes.

Shawn bit his lip.

Was he in big trouble?

Four

Miss Hershey's voice was soft. "Were you passing notes in class?"

"No pass note," Shawn said.

Miss Hershey asked, "Did you write one?"

Shawn was worried. Ronny *had* seen him.

He reached into his jeans pocket. The note for the suggestion box was all folded up. He handed it to Miss Hershey.

Her eyes opened wide. "What's this?" she asked.

Shawn said, "This what I write in class. So sorry."

The teacher opened the note. Her pretty blue eyes scanned the page.

She looked up. "My goodness," she said. "You don't deserve a nickname, Shawn. Not one you don't want. Thank you for telling me about this."

He nodded his head in a half bow. Then he caught himself. "Sorry."

Miss Hershey's smile was warm. "Please don't be bashful about talking to me. I want all my students to feel comfortable at school. Always."

Shawn said, "Thank you." He headed outside.

Several boys were already playing soccer. Ronny was on the field, too.

Shawn stood beside the swings and watched.

Abby ran over to him. "What did Miss Hershey want?"

Shawn said, "We have talk. Miss Hershey very nice teacher."

"I know that," Abby insisted. "But why'd she want to see you?"

Shawn explained about the suggestion box. And about his note.

Abby's eyes started to get shiny in the corners. "Did you tell her who is calling you Fiddlesticks?"

Shawn looked down at his feet. "I not say."

Abby shook her head. "Come on, Shawn, you have to tell her!"

Shawn's eyes were wet, too. He wanted them to be dry. But they kept getting watery.

Shawn ran into the school—right to the boys' room. He washed his face.

Soon, Eric came in, too. He stared at Shawn's face. "You've been crying," he said. "What's wrong?"

"Nothing." Shawn looked away.

"Something *is* wrong!" Eric said.

Just then, Ronny Kitch burst in the door.

Shawn saw him first. He didn't say anything to Ronny. He darted past him and ran into the hallway.

At the drinking fountain, Shawn's heart was pounding.

And quickly, he rubbed his eyes dry.

Five

At lunch later, Shawn sat with Abby and her best friend, Stacy Henry.

Dunkum Mifflin, another Cul-de-Sac Kid, came over and sat with them.

Eric and Jason were having hot lunch. They joined Shawn, Abby, and the others.

Shawn and Abby had their packed lunches from home. Shawn had sprinkled garlic on the sticky rice this morning. He used chopsticks to eat cold *bulgogi* in a plastic dish. The cold Korean beef stir-fry was his favorite lunch.

"Why'd you run away in the boys' room?" Eric asked.

Shawn's mouth was full. He didn't answer.

When he finished chewing, Ronny Kitch had shown up.

"*Ugh!*" Ronny covered his nose. "What's that horrible smell?"

Abby grinned. "It's garlic. And if it bugs you, then go away."

"Yuck! Garlic isn't cool," he roared at Shawn. "Haven't you learned anything since coming here?"

Eric and Jason looked at each other. Their mouths dropped open.

Stacy shook her head.

Dunkum and Abby frowned.

Shawn put his head down. He was afraid Ronny might hit him.

He stared at his chopsticks. He thought about the suggestion box note. What if Ronny knew he'd tattled? What would Ronny do?

Shawn heard Ronny laughing.

"Only sissies play violin," the mean boy said. "And only weirdos eat with chopsticks!"

Jason leaped out of his seat. "Leave Shawn alone!"

"It's not cool to make fun," Eric insisted.

Abby spoke up. "Eric's right. It's not cool." She was frowning.

Shawn was shaking.

"Have you ever heard of the Golden Rule?" Abby asked.

"Sounds dumb," Ronny said. He clumped around the table and stood behind Shawn.

Shawn could feel the heat.

"You can read about the Golden Rule in the Bible," Dunkum said.

Eric said, "Look it up. Matthew 7, verse 12."

Ronny laughed. "No thanks!"

Shawn wished Ronny would go away. His chopsticks were starting to rattle.

Ronny leaned over Shawn. "So . . . how was your chat with Miss Hershey?" he mocked.

Now Jason spoke up. "Get lost, Ronny Kitch!"

"Yeah," Abby said. "Or I'm telling!"

Ronny copied her in a pinched-up voice. "Or I'm telling!"

"I mean it!" Abby said. She got up and headed for the lunchroom monitor.

Shawn wished Abby would hurry back. He wanted her right here. With him.

Ronny stuck out his tongue at Shawn. "How do you like having your sister baby-sit you?"

Then he left.

Shawn put his chopsticks down.

"Ronny's rotten," Jason said.

Eric agreed. "No kidding."

Shawn looked up to see Abby coming back to their table. *Good*, he thought.

"Thank goodness, Ronny's gone," Abby said. She looked at Shawn. "And I think I know who started the nickname."

Shawn said nothing.

"It was Ronny," Abby said. "I'm right, aren't I?"

Shawn felt hot.

He pressed his lips together tight.

Six

The lunchroom was almost empty.

The Cul-de-Sac Kids were still talking.

Abby said, "We can help you, Shawn."

Eric and Jason nodded.

"Abby's right," Jason said.

Dunkum and Stacy looked worried.

"Please tell us," Stacy said.

Finally, Shawn said, "I not want trouble."

"Who does?" Jason said. "But Ronny Kitch is already trouble."

"Big trouble," Eric said. "He pushed me around during recess yesterday. I had the ball. I was dribbling, close to making a goal."

Shawn listened. Anything about soccer, and he was all ears.

"I was ready for a kick to the goal," Eric continued. "But someone shoved me and took the ball away. Guess who?"

Jason was wide-eyed. "Ronny is *not* a team player!"

Eric nodded. "That's the truth."

"And he was on *your* team," Jason said.

"That's the weirdest thing," Eric said.

Shawn listened.

"What happened next?" Abby asked.

Eric's eyes rolled. "Ronny booted the ball. *He* made the goal."

"It should have been yours," Jason said.

"That's how Ronny is," Eric said. "Rotten."

Shawn's jaw twitched. "That not how things be," he said. "Must change!"

Abby's eyes were on him now. "We need to have a long talk," she said. "How about after school?"

"I play violin then," he said.

"How about when you get home?" Abby asked.

Jason smiled. "Good idea. Talk to Abby. She's a good listener."

"Good friend, too," said Stacy. "*Chingu*." She smiled at Shawn.

But Shawn was silent.

■■■

The Cul-de-Sac Kids went out for recess. Abby and Stacy scurried off to the swings. Dunkum and Eric went to shoot hoops.

"Want to play soccer?" Jason asked Shawn.

"Thank you. But no," he answered.

"Aw, come on," Jason said. He looked at the soccer field. "Ronny's not playing."

Shawn checked things out. Jason was right. Ronny was way on the other side of the playground.

It was safe.

"Come on," Jason insisted. "I'll teach you."

Shawn didn't need to be taught. But Jason didn't know that.

Jason begged him to play. "Come on, you'll love it," he said. "I know you will."

Shawn really wanted to play. This would be his first chance to play on this field. The long, beautiful soccer field.

He glanced at the far end of the playground. Ronny was still there.

At last, Shawn agreed. "OK, I play."

Jason started by showing how to dribble. A little at a time.

Shawn dribbled, too. But he kept watch for Ronny.

Jason showed how to rocket the ball to the goal.

Shawn tried. Three times he made it.

Jason shouted, "Goal!" each time.

Shawn was having a great time.

He forgot about Ronny.

"Wow, you're good," Jason said. "Did you play soccer in Korea?"

Shawn grinned. He didn't want Jason to know about his secret practice. "Not in Korea."

Jason seemed surprised. "Let's try some fancy moves."

"I try," Shawn said.

Jason grinned and showed off his fancy footwork.

Shawn was getting the feel of it. He was doing really well.

Suddenly, a shadow fell over him. An enormous shadow. The shadow followed the ball as it rolled downfield.

Jason yelled at the big shadow. "Hey! We had the ball first!"

But Shawn didn't say anything. He kept dribbling. There was no other choice. It was dribble or die.

The shadow was roaring now.

Too close!

Seven

Shawn raced toward the goal area. He still had the ball.

"Fiddlesticks can't play soccer!" the shadow yelled.

Shawn tried to shut out the horrible nickname.

Fiddlesticks.

The name burned like hot peppers.

Shawn couldn't think about the ball. He couldn't think about his feet. And the goal—which way was it?

"Fiddlesticks . . . Fiddlesticks!" the voice shouted.

Shawn knew that voice. It was the put-down voice. That voice kept him awake at night. Sometimes, he heard it in his worst dreams.

Shawn turned around slowly.

Ronny rushed at him like a giant. "Go back where you came from," he sneered.

He kept coming.

Closer.

Shawn was scared stiff. He sped up.

"Don't you understand English, fiddle sticks boy?" Ronny said. "Go back to Korea! I don't want you here!"

Jason caught up. "That's a horrible thing to say."

Ronny stopped running. He turned and looked Jason in the eye. "Don't stick up for Fiddlesticks!" Ronny roared.

"Stop it!" yelled Jason. "Shawn's not Fiddlesticks! He's a *person*!"

Shawn stopped running. He stood very still. He saw the angry glow in Ronny's eyes and was afraid for Jason.

Ronny put up his fists.

Shawn gulped. "Not fight!" he shouted. "Please, not fight!"

Ronny glared at Shawn. "Keep out of this! You got me in trouble with Miss Hershey. You'll be sorry for that!"

Then Ronny spotted the soccer ball. He

shoved Jason aside. He charged down the field toward Shawn.

Zoom!

With a mighty kick, the ball flew across the field.

Ronny roared like a lion. He dribbled a few feet downfield. Then he booted the ball toward the goal.

But the kick was off. Way off. It landed outside the goal box.

Jason started laughing.

Shawn didn't. He was too scared.

Just then, the recess bell rang.

Jason pulled on Shawn's sleeve. "Let's get out of here."

Shawn's face was burning. "You not fight. That good thing."

"*This* time Ronny was lucky," Jason muttered. "I wanted to smash his face."

The boys hurried to the classroom door. They huffed and puffed.

Shawn looked back over his shoulder.

Jason looked back, too.

"Ronny not coming," Shawn said.

"That was close," Jason said. Then he wiped his face on his sleeve. "Hey, you're really good.

You should come practice soccer after school. After violin."

Shawn wanted to. He really did. But Ronny Kitch might be there.

Should he take the chance?

Eight

Ronny bugged Shawn all afternoon. He poked him with a pencil. He kicked his chair. He muttered put-downs.

"You told about the nickname," Ronny whispered. "Miss Hershey scolded me at lunch."

Shawn thought Miss Hershey's talk would change things. But it hadn't. Ronny was still pestering him.

Now Miss Hershey wasn't looking.

Ronny whispered again. "Better watch that dumb violin of yours. It might disappear!"

Shawn curled his toes inside his shoes. Ronny was rotten. Was he a thief, too?

Shawn didn't want to sit near Ronny anymore. He couldn't think about his work. He couldn't think about his violin lesson. And he couldn't think about trying out for soccer!

■ ■ ■

After school, Shawn's violin teacher greeted him. "How are you, Shawn?" asked Mr. Jones.

"I have big surprise," Shawn said.

Mr. Jones's eyes lit up. "What's the surprise?"

"I learn all songs for you," Shawn said.

He tucked his violin under his chin and began to play.

Mr. Jones closed his eyes. He swayed to the music. Sometimes, he stopped to point out soft and loud parts.

When Shawn finished, Mr. Jones smiled. "What a wonderful surprise. You are an excellent violin player."

Shawn bowed low. He wanted to bow— even in America.

After his lesson, Shawn hurried to the soccer field. He looked for Jason and Eric. They were nowhere in sight. Ronny Kitch was. Right in the middle of everything.

Quickly, Shawn turned away. He gripped

his violin case and remembered what Ronny had said. *Better watch your violin.*

"No soccer for me," Shawn said out loud.

"Why not?" a voice called.

Shawn spun around.

It was Jason Birchall.

"Hi," Shawn said. He was glad to see his friend.

"You're staying, aren't you?" Jason asked.

"Well . . . uh . . ." Shawn looked down at his violin. He wanted to stay and play soccer. He really did. But he didn't want to lose his violin. His wonderful, beautiful instrument. Ronny might steal it out from under his nose!

Just then, Coach spotted Shawn. "Welcome!" he called and kicked a ball to him.

Shawn stopped the ball with his foot. But he held on to his violin case.

"Come on!" hollered Jason. He was already running down the field.

So was Coach.

Shawn dribbled around the edge of the field. Far away from Ronny. His violin was safe with him.

He punted back and forth with Jason. Then he rocketed the ball toward the goal.

"Hey, good stuff!" hollered Jason.

Now Eric was there, too. "Glad you showed up," he said. Then he stared at the violin. "Why are you carrying your instrument around?"

Shawn ran to get the ball.

Jason called to him, "It's not a good idea. Your violin might get crunched."

Shawn thought about it. He loved his violin. He was good at it. The music made him feel terrific.

"I keep violin with me," Shawn said. He held up the case and grinned. "I run with music."

Suddenly, Ronny was coming at him.

Fast!

Shawn didn't have time to protect his violin.

He closed his eyes and prayed.

His violin was about to be history.

So was he!

Nine

Whoosh! Ronny flew past Shawn.

"Fiddlesticks!" Ronny whispered into the wind.

Shawn heard the nickname. He almost dropped his violin case. He gripped harder.

Seconds later, Ronny turned around. He charged at Shawn again. "Fiddlesticks should never play soccer!" he hissed.

Shawn wanted to bop him. Flatten him good!

But the nickname mixed him up. He couldn't remember what to do with his feet.

His ball spun away. It was loose at midfield.

Ronny laughed. "Fiddlesticks!"

Shawn was still carrying his violin. He

looked down. He thought, *This case very hard. Make good head bopper.*

He scanned the field. The coach was at the other end—out of sight. He would never see Ronny getting bopped!

Shawn raised his violin case. His heart thumped.

"Don't!" yelled Eric from the goal.

Ronny punted a ball off his head. "You'll be sorry if you hit me!" he shouted at Shawn.

Ka-boink! Ronny's ball bounced off Shawn's violin case. On purpose.

Shawn saw Eric dashing toward him. "Don't fight back!" Eric yelled. "Remember the Golden Rule."

Just then, Coach came running. He nabbed Ronny. He lugged him right off the field.

Ronny roared and ranted.

Jason laughed. "What a big baby!"

Shawn agreed, but he didn't say anything. He felt awful. He'd almost hit Ronny.

He'd come so close.

■ ■ ■

At home, Shawn and Abby had a long talk. Abby read Matthew 7:12 out loud.

"Read very slow," Shawn said.

Abby did. "'Do for other people the same things you want them to do for you,'" she read.

"Gold rule?" Shawn asked.

"The *Golden* Rule," Abby told him. "One of the most important rules of all."

Shawn thought about the Bible verse. He thought about Ronny Kitch.

"Ronny not know rule?" he asked.

Abby shook her head. "I guess not."

"I teach," Shawn said. "I teach Ronny Golden Rule."

Abby looked surprised. "What do you mean?"

"You see," Shawn said.

"Be careful around Ronny," Abby said. "He could easily beat you up."

"I get strong," Shawn said. He stood up. "And you help me."

He went outside. Abby followed.

"No more fiddle stick legs. No more jelly bean muscles," Shawn explained.

He knelt down in the grass. He started with push-ups. Next came sit-ups. Shawn ran around the backyard while Abby timed him.

"Now measure," Shawn said. He wanted Abby to see if his arms were bigger. His legs, too.

Abby found the measuring tape.

He hadn't grown.

■ ■ ■

The second day, Shawn ran and jumped some more. He did twenty sit-ups. He groaned through fifteen push-ups.

Abby measured his muscles. "No change," she said.

Every day Shawn did his exercises. For two whole weeks!

He ate more food than usual. More American food, too. Pizza and cheeseburgers.

Ice cream and cake.

And lots of celery with creamy dips.

The day before soccer tryouts, Abby measured Shawn's muscles. "They're the same size," she said.

Shawn frowned. "What go wrong?"

Abby tried to explain. "Building up your body takes time. Two weeks isn't enough. Keep exercising."

Shawn sat on the porch step. His face

drooped. "I still Fiddlesticks. I always be Fiddlesticks."

"That's not true!" Abby sat beside him. "You're Shawn Hunter. Don't call yourself Fiddlesticks anymore!"

Shawn was quiet.

So was Abby.

Brr-eep! a cricket chirped.

Buzz-za biz-z-z, bees hummed.

At last, Shawn said, "Maybe I supposed to be small."

"Small isn't so bad," Abby said.

Then Shawn had an idea. "I be fast! Fastest small person in world!"

Abby grinned. "That's a double dabble good idea."

"Tomorrow, I be fastest player on soccer field!"

Shawn couldn't wait for tryouts.

Ten

That night, Shawn packed away his chopsticks.

"I use fork now," he said at supper. "Like other Hunters."

Abby smiled.

So did the rest of the family.

"Only if you want to," Mrs. Hunter said.

After supper, Shawn helped Abby load the dishwasher. When they were finished, he asked her to pray. "I want God to help."

"In making the soccer team?" Abby asked.

Shawn nodded. He pointed to himself. "About skinny body, too."

Abby smiled. "God won't make you big

overnight. He makes our bodies grow, but we can't be in a hurry."

Shawn frowned. "I need big, power body now. I in very big hurry," he said.

"Try to be happy with who you are," Abby said and looked at Shawn. "But I'll pray about tryouts."

Shawn's eyes shone. "I like that. Very much!"

Abby prayed. At the end, she said, "Amen."

"Amen," Shawn said. "I go now. Thank you for prayer."

He went to his room. There, he took out a picture. He sat on the floor beside his dog. Snow White nuzzled into his lap.

Shawn's Korean parents were in the picture. He studied it.

"Father not have power body," he said.

Just then, Jimmy, his little brother, came in. Shawn hid the picture behind his back.

Jimmy found his skates and left.

Shawn sighed. He looked at the picture again. He missed his parents. His father had died years ago. Then his mother became sick. She couldn't take care of Shawn and Jimmy anymore.

Shawn put his arms around Snow White. She licked away his tears.

Shawn hugged her. "You very good pet," he said. "You Golden Rule dog!"

Eleven

It was Friday. Soccer tryout day!

Shawn got up early. He took a warm shower.

Before he dressed, Shawn measured his arms. He hadn't grown overnight. No power body.

Abby was right.

But Shawn knew he could be fast. Faster than the other boys. Even faster than Ronny Kitch!

■■■

Freeet! Coach blew his whistle.

The boys lined up.

"Show me some teamwork," Coach said.

Jason, Eric, and two other boys burst onto the field.

Shawn watched eagerly. They did lots of passing and shooting. Back and forth.

He waited his turn, holding his violin. He didn't dare put it down. Not with Ronny around.

Just then, Ronny came over. "Taking care of that stupid thing?"

Shawn didn't answer.

"Are you deaf, fiddle sticks boy?" Ronny demanded.

Shawn paid no attention. He thought of the Golden Rule and fished a candy bar from his pocket.

"You like?" Shawn held up the candy.

Ronny frowned at first. Then his eyes blinked. He snatched up the candy. "Give me that!"

And off he ran.

Shawn felt inside his pants pocket. He smiled. There was plenty more candy. He was ready for Ronny.

His plan was good. A golden plan.

"Shawn Hunter!" the coach called.

He was next.

The coach glanced at Shawn's violin. A thin smile crossed his face. Then he looked away.

One kid shouted, "Hey, look! Shawn's trying out with a violin!"

Coach waved his hand. "It's music month, right?"

Kids on the sidelines snickered.

"Teamwork!" yelled the coach. He blew his whistle again. "Heads up. Spread out."

Four players rushed onto the field. All of them wanted to be on the team. But none of them more than Shawn.

Things got off to a swift start. Shawn dribbled and passed rapidly. The others scrambled to keep up. Down the field they flew. Clutching his violin, Shawn eased in and out of the players.

"Go, Shawn, go!" Jason shouted.

Fast as he could, Shawn worked his way down the field.

His teammates shot the ball to him, and he stopped it with his foot. He dribbled a few yards. He remembered Jason's fancy footwork. And tried it out.

He was approaching the goal area.

The goalkeeper was guarding like a hawk.

Shawn had to trick him. How?

Teamwork, he thought.

Shawn passed to another player. That player dribbled to the left, then booted it back.

Shawn stopped the ball with his hip and took control.

Pow! He snapped a clean shot into the net.

"Goal!" someone shouted.

Kids chanted on the sidelines. "Go, Fiddlesticks, go!"

The coach blew his whistle. Long and loud.

The crowd got quiet.

"Next group!" Coach said.

Tryouts were over for Shawn. He felt good about his passing and shooting. But mostly he felt glad about his speed.

Jason and Eric circled Shawn.

"You were great!" Jason said.

"He sure was!" Abby said, running up to them.

"You great, too," Shawn said to his cul-de-sac friends.

Eric scratched his head. "How can you play soccer and carry a violin?"

Shawn replied, "Not easy." He smiled so big, his eyes winked shut.

Jason asked, "Hey, what were those kids chanting?"

Shawn tossed his head. He knew. It was the nickname.

"Something about fiddles, I think," Eric said. "Maybe that's because Shawn's so good at violin."

Abby wrinkled up her nose. "Just forget it, OK?"

"Fiddlesticks," Shawn offered. "Kids call me Fiddlesticks."

Abby's eyes nearly popped.

Shawn shook his head. "Nickname not bother me now. Fiddlesticks good name."

Ronny looked their way. He didn't come barging over. But Shawn knew he'd heard what Shawn said.

"Ronny learn golden things," Shawn said softly.

Abby frowned. "What do you mean?"

Shawn thought about the Golden Rule. But he kept quiet.

The kids walked toward Blossom Hill Lane. They talked about soccer and the team list.

"When will we know who made it?" Jason asked.

"Monday, after school," Eric said.

"A whole weekend to wait," Abby chanted.

Jason jigged down the cul-de-sac. "Wouldn't it be cool if we all made the team?"

"Very cool," said Shawn.

But he was thinking about Ronny. Would *he* make the team, too?

Twelve

Monday finally came.

The team list was posted high on the gym door.

Shawn stood on tiptoes, reading the bottom names first. He saw Jason's name. And Eric's.

Shawn kept going, reading *up* the list.

"Hey," called Jason. "Did you make the team?"

Shawn was still reading. "*You* make team," he said.

Jason started to dance in the hall.

Shawn made his eyes squint. But the names at the top of the list were too far away. He couldn't see them.

The school bell rang. Kids hurried to class.

"Come on," called Jason. "We'll be late."

Shawn turned to go. He wished he could see the top names. Maybe his was up there. Maybe not.

■■■

Miss Hershey called the roll.

After that, she passed around some papers.

Shawn read his right away. *Very good*, he thought. *Music homework*.

"We're going to do something special for Bach's birthday," Miss Hershey said. "We're going to have a Bach Bash."

Some of the kids had forgotten who Bach was. Miss Hershey reminded them of the famous music composer. Then she handed out ideas for creative reports.

Shawn raised his hand. "I play Bach piece on violin, yes?"

Miss Hershey smiled. "I hoped you would want to play," she said. "Thank you, Shawn."

All morning, Ronny was kind. He didn't poke Shawn. He kept his feet to himself. He didn't say the nickname.

The class got busy. They divided into groups. Ronny was in Shawn's group.

Miss Hershey came around and listened to each group. But Ronny was silent. He let Shawn do all the talking.

Shawn was surprised. What a big change. It was a Ronny Kitch switch!

■■■

During recess, Shawn and Jason went to the gym. They looked at the soccer list.

Jason spotted Shawn's name. "You made it!" he cried.

Shawn jumped up to see his name. It was at the top of the list. But he kept looking. "I not see Ronny on list," he said.

Jason shook his head. "Ronny didn't make the team this year."

"He not?" Shawn asked.

"Coach heard about the nickname," Jason said. "He didn't like the way Ronny was acting."

Jason ran out for recess.

Shawn hurried to catch up, but inside, he felt sad. Sad for Ronny.

Shawn played on the soccer field with the other boys. Ronny watched from the sidelines.

Then Shawn had an idea. Another golden one. He marched off the field. Right up to Ronny.

"You want candy?" he asked.

Ronny's face turned happy. "Are you kidding? After what I called you? After what I did?"

Shawn gave him an eyeball gumball. "For you from Fiddlesticks."

Ronny's mouth dropped two feet. "What did you say?"

"You not deaf. You hear right," Shawn said. "Fiddlesticks nickname good. Make me run fast. Make me feel like music."

Ronny shook his head. "I don't believe this."

"Believe," Shawn said. "Good thing, to believe."

He thought of the Golden Rule.

And he smiled.

BOOK 12

The Crabby
Cat Caper

For Janet Huntington,
who draws the pictures
in these books
and
who lives with
two very crabby cats—
Nancy and Little John.

One

"Yucko," said Dee Dee Winters. "Thinking up riddles is hard."

She stared out her bedroom window. She tapped her pencil on the desk.

It was almost summer. The last day of May.

Two weeks till summer vacation.

Three days till the school carnival.

Meow. Mister Whiskers curled against Dee Dee's legs.

"I have to write a riddle for school," she told him. "Any ideas?"

Merrrt. Mister Whiskers shook his furry body. His name tag jingled.

"Don't tell me no," Dee Dee said. "You haven't even tried."

Mister Whiskers found a sunny spot on the floor. He licked his sleek, gray coat.

His whiskers wiggled. They waggled.

Purrr. The sound was like a motorboat. A soft, distant one.

"Is that all you have to say?" Dee Dee rolled her dark eyes. "You're no help."

Mister Whiskers stretched his soft body against the carpet.

"So . . . just like that, you're taking a nap?" Dee Dee said.

The long whiskers twitched. Dreamland was on its way.

What can I expect? she thought. *He's a cat. A crabby little cat.*

She was right. Mister Whiskers was definitely crabby. Sometimes worse than crabby. Sometimes he took risks.

Big ones!

Daring thrills and certain chills.

Potted plant spills from windowsills.

Sometimes he set off fire drills.

That's what Mister Whiskers was all about.

Dee Dee picked up her pencil. She decided to try to write the riddle again.

"Everyone in class has to write one," Dee

Dee explained to her sleepy cat. "The riddle is due Monday."

She checked her kitty calendar. The May border had cat paws along the side.

"This is Friday afternoon," Dee Dee said. "I better hurry."

Mew. Mister Whiskers opened one droopy eye.

"You agree with me? Well, it's about time." Dee Dee laughed.

She picked up her pencil. She wrote:

A Riddle
by
Dee Dee Winters

She stopped. "Now what? What comes next?"

Mister Whiskers didn't open his eyes this time. The cozy cat was somewhere in snooze land. Probably dreaming about his supper. Or his next adventure.

Dee Dee made kissy noises.

No response.

"Fine and dandy," she whispered. "Sleep your life away."

But Dee Dee didn't want Mister Whiskers to sleep. Not at all. She wanted his eyes wide open. She wanted his tail jerking.

Dee Dee wanted company. Someone to talk to. Even if it was only cat chat!

Two

Dee Dee started to write again. But her pencil was dull. She went to her pencil sharpener. All the while, she was thinking about her riddle.

"I've got it!" she said at last. "I know what I'll write!" Dee Dee hurried to her desk.

Neatly, she printed these words:

> *I am green.*
> *I make a certain cat hiss.*
> *I have blinking eyes and eat flies.*
> *Who am I?*
> *Hint: My name starts with C.*

She put her pencil down and read the riddle and the hint. She thought about it.

Then she read it again. This time out loud.

Dee Dee wasn't sure if she liked it. "Everyone will know the answer," she said. "It's too easy."

She thought about Jason Birchall's frog, Croaker. The bullfrog made her cat go crazy. Totally goofy.

The Cul-de-Sac Kids were going to take pets to the school carnival. They wanted to walk around and show them off.

Yesterday, they'd had a big meeting about it. A Cul-de-Sac Kids meeting. All pet decisions had been made.

Stacy Henry was taking Sunday Funnies, her white cockapoo. Dunkum Mifflin was putting a leash on his rabbit, Blinkee.

Eric Hagel was taking Fran the Ham, his girl hamster. He would carry her around in his shirt pocket.

Shawn Hunter was taking Snow White, his floppy-eared puppy. Carly and Jimmy Hunter wanted to take their pet ducks, Quacker and Jack.

Ducks at a carnival? thought Dee Dee.

She had nearly burst out laughing. How could that possibly work? But she'd kept quiet at the meeting.

And there was Croaker to think about.

She'd asked Jason to keep his bullfrog home. "Don't frogs need to be in water?"

At first, Jason argued. "You're just saying that because you don't want Mister Whiskers to have a hissy fit."

"You're right," she said. "So *please* keep your frog at home!"

Jason had pouted.

But Dee Dee won him over. "I'll make some cookies."

"My favorite?" Jason asked.

Jason wasn't supposed to eat chocolate. It wound him up. But carob-chip cookies tasted a lot like chocolate-chip cookies.

"I'll bring them to school on Monday," Dee Dee said.

So it was settled.

Mister Whiskers could attend the carnival *purr*fectly happy. And Croaker would stay home in his aquarium.

Where he belongs, thought Dee Dee.

She stood up and looked out the window. From her bedroom, she could see Blossom Hill School. Jason's father and some other men were working. They were building the booths for the carnival.

"I can't wait till Monday," Dee Dee said. "The carnival will be so much fun!"

She turned to look at her cat.

But Mister Whiskers was gone.

"Where'd you go?" Dee Dee said.

She searched under her bed. It was Mister Whiskers' favorite hiding spot. "Here kitty, kitty," she called.

No cat.

She ran downstairs to the kitchen.

Maybe he's hungry, she thought.

But Mister Whiskers wasn't eating from his dish. He wasn't drinking milk from his bowl, either.

"Where *are* you?" she cried.

She checked under the lamp table. Sometimes he curled up there.

Today, he wasn't there.

She searched all the windowsills. Especially the ones with potted plants.

No Mister Whiskers.

Where could he be? she thought.

Then she had an idea.

Maybe he'd gotten out. He liked to run loose in the cul-de-sac. He was always running away.

The back screen door hung open some-times. It had to be tugged hard to give it a snug fit.

Eagerly, Dee Dee checked the front and back doors. They were shut tight. There was no way for Mister Whiskers to escape. Not today.

Dee Dee was stumped. Her cat had tricked her.

"You'll be sorry!" she hollered up the steps. "You won't get your afternoon cookie."

She sat down on the living room floor.

Under her breath, she counted. "One . . . two . . . three . . . four . . ."

Before she got to five, Mister Whiskers came. He padded down the steps, looking shy. A little uneasy, too.

Dee Dee saw bits of paper around his mouth. "What have you been doing?" she said.

Meow. Mister Whiskers stared at her with his sly yellow-orange eyes. Slowly, he blinked.

"Come here, you!" She picked the pieces out of his whiskers.

Finally, all the bits of paper were in the trash.

Dee Dee remembered the way her cat had

blinked at her. Something else had eyes like that. Well, sort of.

Croaker, Jason's bullfrog, had tricky eyes, too.

"You stay right here." Dee Dee wagged her finger in his furry face. "Don't you dare move!"

She ran upstairs. She ran so fast, her hair bow fell off.

Dee Dee was determined. She was going to find out what trouble Mister Whiskers had been up to.

Right now!

Three

Dee Dee scurried to her bedroom. Slowly, she scanned the room with her eyes.

Then she spotted it. Plain as day.

There, on the floor, were pieces of shredded paper. Right beside her desk.

"Why, that little crab cake!" Dee Dee muttered. "He tore up my riddle."

Then she remembered. The riddle was about Croaker. She'd read it out loud.

But she thought Mister Whiskers hadn't heard it. She thought he was sound asleep.

He tricked me again, she thought.

Dee Dee dashed downstairs. "You really don't like that bullfrog, do you?" she said.

Merrrt, the furry face replied. It was cat chat for *Nope*.

"Well, I don't blame you," Dee Dee said. "But that doesn't mean you can rip up my riddle."

Mister Whiskers slinked down. Like he was going to pounce on a mouse.

"OK, that does it," Dee Dee said. "Crabby cats don't sleep in *my* room. Downstairs—to the cellar!"

Meoorsy?

"That's right, the cellar," she insisted.

Mister Whiskers hated the cellar. It was dark, musty, and lonely.

No people.

No soft beds.

No canned tuna!

Mister Whiskers' face suddenly changed. No more sly look. Not the uneasy-looking one, either. The kind that said, *I'm in trouble!*

Now the cat mouth was turned down. The eyelids drooped to narrow slits. A very sour look ruled his face.

Dee Dee tore into him. "What a crab cake you are! Why don't you behave yourself?"

He whined and spit like he'd been kicked.

Dee Dee said, "You must learn a hard lesson."

She leaned over to pick him up.

Whoosh! Mister Whiskers flew out of her reach.

"Hey!" she shouted. "Come back here!"

Dee Dee chased her cat around the living room.

Mister Whiskers darted into the dining room. And sailed under the table. He weaved through the maze of chair legs. Always, just out of her reach.

"Mister Whiskers!" she squealed. "Stop!"

But it was no use. Her cat was angry.

Cellars were for dogs. And garbage cans. Cats deserved far better.

Dee Dee was almost certain those were Mister Whiskers' thoughts.

Out of breath, she stopped trailing him. She sat down on one of the dining room chairs.

A great idea popped into her head, and she began to smile.

"Want to bake some cookies?" she called. "Here, kitty, kitty . . . cookie." That would surely bring him running.

Fast as a mouse, Mister Whiskers jumped up on her lap. He licked his chops. He looked so cute—eyes all perky. Tail all swishy.

As she stared at him, Dee Dee felt sorry. Her great idea fell flat. She couldn't banish Mister Whiskers to the cellar.

Not now. Not later.

"Aw, you silly crab cake," she said. And Dee Dee kissed his soft little head.

Meoorry.

"I know you're sorry," she said. "Now, let's bake Jason's cookies. He'll keep his frog home from the carnival if we do." She grinned at her cat. "Then *you* can go with me."

Mister Whiskers seemed pleased. He puffed out his body and nuzzled Dee Dee's face.

"Want to help?"

She didn't have to ask twice. Dee Dee knew her cat well. Very well.

Four

After supper, Mrs. Winters served dessert. Dee Dee carried in a bowl of peaches. Next came some whipped cream—the real stuff.

"Yummers!" she said.

Mister Whiskers was perched on the floor beside her chair. His eyes were on the sweet whipped cream.

"I made carob-chip cookies today," Dee Dee announced. "My cat and I did."

Her father's eyes danced. "Sounds delicious."

Dee Dee set a plateful of cookies on the kitchen table. "We made extra," she said.

Her mother smiled. "You must have cooked up something with your cul-de-sac friends."

Dee Dee nodded. "Jason wanted to take his frog to the school carnival. But if he did, then I couldn't take Mister Whiskers."

Her father looked up. "Why not?"

"Because my cat hates that frog," she said.

"Well, seems to me your cat pretty much runs things around here," her father said.

"I know," Dee Dee said. "But he's so cute and cuddly."

But she knew Mister Whiskers was also a cranky, crabby cat. That's why he got his way. Most of the time.

"Anyway, we made the cookies for Jason," Dee Dee explained. "He won't mind leaving his frog home."

Her parents traded glances.

Dee Dee noticed. "Well, I *am* being nice to Jason," she said. "Not mean like Mister Whiskers is sometimes."

"Not just sometimes," her father said. "That cat is a real pain *most* of the time."

Dee Dee reached down and tickled Mister Whiskers' neck. She hoped he hadn't heard.

■■■

After supper, Dee Dee played with her cat. She scratched his left ear. Mister Whiskers liked it there best.

"You did a good job today," she said. "You licked the cookie bowl nice and clean."

Meoow-mew.

"You're welcome," Dee Dee said. "Now I have to write my riddle for school."

She carried the cat upstairs. "Promise not to eat my homework this time?"

Mister Whiskers was quiet.

"Oh, you're not making any promises, is that it?" Dee Dee sighed. She frisked Mister Whiskers' chin.

"To be truthful, I didn't like the bullfrog riddle, either," she told her cat.

Dee Dee picked up her pencil. She set to work.

Mister Whiskers helped, too. He helped by settling into a cozy spot. Right on Dee Dee's bed.

It sure beat the cellar. Any day!

Five

The next day was Saturday.

Dee Dee's doorbell rang after breakfast.

Mister Whiskers was sunning himself. He liked to sit by the living room window.

The doorbell rang. He sniffed the air like he could almost smell a bullfrog.

Dee Dee opened the door.

"Hi, Jason," she said.

Jason hopped around a bit. Then he said, "I came over for my cookies."

Dee Dee frowned. "That's not what we agreed on."

"I don't care," he said. "I can't wait till Monday. I want them *now*."

"Well, too bad." Dee Dee reached for the doorknob.

Jason stuck his foot in the door. "The deal's off. I'm taking Croaker to the carnival."

With that, he pulled his bullfrog out of his jacket.

Mister Whiskers spied the frog. In a flash, he leaped off his window perch.

Hiss! Phttt! He was going goofy.

"Get your cat away!" Jason hollered. "I mean it!"

Just then, Mrs. Winters came into the living room. "What on earth is going on?"

She saw Jason holding his bullfrog.

"Uh, Jason," she said, "would you mind stepping outside with that uh . . . uh . . ."

"This is Croaker." He held the bullfrog high.

Mrs. Winters waved her hands. "Please take him outside!"

By now, Mister Whiskers was having a royal fit. He spread his long claws. He even tried to follow Jason and his bullfrog outside.

But Jason backed away. "I . . . I have to go help my dad now," he said. "Bye, Dee Dee!"

With a great burst of speed, he rushed down the front steps.

Mister Whiskers pushed his nose against the screen door. Still fussing at Croaker.

Dee Dee caught him just in time. "Oh, no you don't," she said. "You're not going near that frog!"

The cat's eyes squinted into a sly slant.

Merrrt! He leaped up onto his sunny sill.

■■■

Mister Whiskers sat tall. King of kitties.

With hope in his eyes, he watched Jason walk across the street. He saw him head for the school. He knew the bullfrog was in Jason's pocket.

The sun began to warm Mister Whiskers again. He relaxed, washing his paws in the sunlight.

Soon, he began to daydream. His kitty dream was filled with sweet freedom. He could almost taste the green grass. A young, juicy field mouse . . .

Purrr. Mister Whiskers snoozed. Running away was his best dream yet.

The hot sun poured through the bay window.

He was bigger than a mountain lion. He

could outrun anything. Mice and dogs. Even a bullfrog!

Only inches to go. He was that close to catching the ugly green frog. . . .

■■■

"Wake up, kitty," Dee Dee called.

She went to the windowsill. Gently, she picked him up and carried him to the kitchen.

"Time for some din-din."

Her cat yawned and stretched.

"Oh, you poor thing. You're so tired," Dee Dee said. She put him down. He could hardly stand up.

Then she opened the fridge. "Cold milk will perk you up." She turned her back, still cooing to her cat.

But someone had forgotten to tug on the back screen door. It was hanging open a crack.

Just enough.

Six

Dee Dee stood in the middle of the kitchen. She couldn't believe her eyes.

"Mister Whiskers was right here!" she explained to her mother.

"He'll come back," Mrs. Winters said.

Dee Dee went to the back door and looked out. *He's a house cat*, she thought. *He needs to be indoors.*

She turned to her mother. "Mister Whiskers has always wanted his freedom," she said. "I can tell by the look in his eyes."

She sniffled.

Mrs. Winters slipped her arm around Dee Dee. "Don't worry, honey."

But Dee Dee *was* worried. She was very worried.

What if Mister Whiskers didn't want to come home?

What then?

■ ■ ■

Later, Dee Dee helped her father sweep the porch.

"I don't want to wait for Mister Whiskers to come home," she said. "I want to go find him."

Mr. Winters nodded with a grunt. Then he went to get the garden hose.

"I'm gonna look for him," Dee Dee said. "As soon as I'm finished here."

"OK with me," Mr. Winters mumbled. He began to hose down the front porch.

Dee Dee knew her dad wasn't very worried. Maybe he was secretly glad.

"Do you miss our cat?" she asked.

"Miss who?" he said. "*Our* cat?"

"Well, you know," Dee Dee said softly.

She wished her dad thought of Mister Whiskers that way. She wished he thought of the cat as family.

At last, Dee Dee's chores were done. She set off down the cul-de-sac.

First, she stopped at Jason Birchall's house next door.

"My cat ran off," she told Jason's mother.

"I'm sorry to hear that," Mrs. Birchall said. "I'll tell Jason to watch for him."

"Thanks," said Dee Dee.

She went to Eric Hagel's house. He lived in the house next to Jason. Eric's grandpa was sitting on the porch.

"Have you seen my cat?" Dee Dee asked.

Grandpa Hagel yawned. "Can't say that I have."

"If you see him, will you let me know?" she asked.

The old man nodded. "I'd be glad to."

Mr. Tressler lived at the very end of Blossom Hill Lane. Dee Dee headed there next.

She rang the doorbell.

Seconds passed, and Mr. Tressler opened the door. "Hello there, little missy," he said. "What can I do for you?"

"Just hoped you'd seen my cat."

Mr. Tressler leaned on his cane. "He ran off, eh?"

Dee Dee nodded. "I think he wants his freedom."

"Could be," he said. "But a well-fed pet always returns."

"Really?" she said. This was good news.

"Yes, indeedy." Mr. Tressler jiggled his cane.

"So . . . Mister Whiskers will come home!" She scampered down the opposite side of the cul-de-sac. It was Stacy Henry's side of the street.

She turned to go toward Stacy's house. But stopped. "Wait a minute," she said out loud. "A well-fed pet always comes home. Mr. Tressler said so."

So she decided not to bother looking. Her cat could come dragging home when he was ready. Probably around suppertime.

I'll go help at the carnival, she thought.

And that's what she did.

■■■

Much later, Dee Dee poured milk into Mister Whiskers' bowl. She set it outside near the back door.

"This'll bring him back," she said.

Her mother agreed. "Good idea."

Dee Dee waited and watched. She waited some more.

She waited till supper.

No cat.

She waited till *after* supper.

No Mister Whiskers.

She waited till bedtime.

Nothing.

She tiptoed downstairs after her mother had tucked her in.

Still no sign of her cat.

Dee Dee unhooked the back screen door. She let it hang open. Just enough.

She sat on the floor, waiting. She waited till the moon slid over Jason's roof next door.

But Mister Whiskers didn't come home.

That crab cake! thought Dee Dee.

Seven

Dee Dee got up early Sunday morning. She dashed downstairs.

The screen door was locked now. She unlatched it and went outside.

She checked the kitty bowl. Sour milk.

"Yuck!" She dumped it out.

Back inside, she woke up her parents. "Mister Whiskers didn't come home," Dee Dee told them.

Her father rolled over. He made husky early morning sounds under the covers.

Her mother sat up. She stroked Dee Dee's hair. "Oh, he'll come home. You'll see."

Dee Dee kept watch for her cat. Even after breakfast. And between teeth brushing and getting ready for church.

Soon, it was time to leave for Sunday school.

During prayer time, Dee Dee talked to God. "Please take care of my cat," she whispered.

■■■

After dinner, Dee Dee went to see Carly Hunter. She and Carly were best friends.

She told Carly about her runaway cat. "I hope he comes back real soon," she said sadly.

"Me too," Carly said. "It would be lonely at your house without him."

Dee Dee sighed. "My dad doesn't think so. He'd probably care more if we got a dog."

Carly giggled. "How can you say that?"

"Some people like dogs best," Dee Dee replied. "I think my dad's a dog person."

Carly played with her long curls. "Dogs aren't better than cats." She turned to look at Dee Dee. "Did you ask God to help you find him?"

Dee Dee nodded. "At church."

"Then don't worry," Carly suggested.

Dee Dee smiled. "OK, I'll try not to."

And she did try.

She tried so hard, she almost forgot about Mister Whiskers.

■■■

On Monday, she gave Jason his cookies. At lunch, the kids talked about the carnival. Jason was busy eating his carob-chip cookies.

After recess, Dee Dee turned in her riddle. It went like this:

A Riddle
by
Dee Dee Winters

I help bake cookies.
And eat them, too.
Sometimes, I act like a crab cake.
I speak a secret language.
And I love freedom!
Who am I?
Clue: none

Dee Dee didn't bother telling Jason that her cat was still missing.

After school, the Cul-de-Sac Kids met at Abby's house.

Abby Hunter was the president of the club. "We don't have to have another meeting, do we?" she asked.

No one wanted another meeting. They were too excited about the carnival.

"Double dabble good," Abby said. "No meeting. Let's go!"

They made a circle and locked hands. "Cul-de-Sac Kids stick together," they chanted.

At the end of their block, they crossed the street together. Kids and pets.

Abby Hunter was the only one without a pet. Dee Dee Winters had one, but it was absent—a runaway.

Jason Birchall chomped on his cookies— the perfect reward for leaving his frog behind. Only now, with Mister Whiskers gone, he could have brought Croaker along, Dee Dee thought.

But she decided not to say anything. Jason would probably figure it out.

Soon, the Cul-de-Sac Kids were exploring the carnival. They showed off their pets.

"It's a pet parade," Jason said to Dee Dee. "Remember the one we had last Easter?"

Dee Dee remembered.

Suddenly, Jason's eyes grew big. "Hey!" he shouted.

"What's wrong?" Dee Dee asked.

"Your cat's not here," he said. "So why can't Croaker come to the carnival?"

Dee Dee couldn't think of a reason. Well, she could. But she didn't want to cause trouble. Not now. Not here at the carnival.

"I want to show off my pet!" Jason said.

"Then go home and get him," Dee Dee replied.

And with that, Jason left the school grounds. He ran all the way home.

Dee Dee hoped he was doing the right thing. What if the other pets starting hissing at Croaker?

But she knew she didn't have to worry. Dogs and ducks couldn't care less about bullfrogs. Neither could rabbits and hamsters.

Cats were the ones who hissed and spit. They had hissy fits. At least, Mister Whiskers always did.

But today, Dee Dee wouldn't have to worry about her crabby cat. Mister Whiskers was gone. Having a long taste of freedom.

He was far away from home by now. Maybe many miles away.

Eight

The House of Mirrors was a frightful place. A place for scaredy-cats.

Mister Whiskers opened one eye. Bravely, he took another peek. He was as big as a mountain lion. This was not a dream!

He stared at the strange mirror. Both eyes wide. That face . . . and those ears. Had he always looked this way?

Suddenly, he heard voices. A familiar voice stood out. It was Dee Dee's, his favorite girl-person.

Merrrt! Mister Whiskers couldn't let her find him. Not now. Not yet!

There were too many wonderful smells and sounds. He was enjoying freedom. And people food!

Since running away, he'd begun to understand life on the outside. Now he knew why
humans ate junk food.

Mm-m-meoowsy! Scraps of French fries
and bits of hot dog. And melted ice cream
on wrappers.

Mister Whiskers loved his new life!

But he hid when Dee Dee and her friends
came near. He slinked away, out of sight. He
crawled behind the tallest mirror.

Dee Dee and Carly posed in front of the
fat mirror. They were giggling and talking.

"Let's tell Jason to bring Croaker in here,"
Carly said.

Dee Dee grinned. "That bullfrog will look
fatter than ever!"

The girls tried out the tall, skinny mirror.
And all the others.

When they left, they were still laughing.

Mister Whiskers felt something tickle his
insides. A homesick bug, maybe?

Or was it the junk food?

Suddenly a familiar scent hit his nose. He
sniffed the air.

The muscles in his furry body froze. The
hair on his back stood in a ridge.

He sniffed again. What was that horrid smell?

Then he knew. His claws shot out.

FROG!

Mister Whiskers crept close to the ground. He slinked under the tall mirror. He wanted to find that bullfrog.

He *had* to find him!

Mister Whiskers peeked out from under the tall mirror. He spied himself—a very fat self—a few feet away. In the fat mirror.

Jason was holding his bullfrog in front of the fat mirror, too.

Ribbit! Croaker spotted Mister Whiskers! The bullfrog leaped out of Jason's hands.

"What?" Jason said, spinning around.

Boink, boink! The frog hopped out of the House of Mirrors. He headed for the dunk tank.

The principal was sitting in the dunking chair. He sat high above the water.

Whee! Croaker leaped up and flew over the fence. He splashed down, into the water tank.

Mister Whiskers was close behind. He tried to make the fence.

Splaaat! Not quite.

He fell to the ground, staring at the fence. He hissed at his poor judgment.

Then he heard a sound. *Quack, quackity-quack!*

Quacker and Jack were loose. They were waddling toward him. Their thin rope leashes dragged behind.

Merrrt! Mister Whiskers didn't like the looks of those long beaks. He arched his back.

But nope, it wasn't worth a fit. Those slow-poke ducks would never catch him.

He turned his attention back to the bull-frog.

Croaker was swimming around, having a good time. Safe inside the dunk tank!

Mister Whiskers stared at him. Could *he* swim today? Should he risk one of his nine lives?

Suddenly, out of the corner of his eye, he saw a fluff of white. Snow White, Shawn's dog, was charging at him!

Zoom! Mister Whiskers darted away from the dunk tank. He zipped toward the food stand, under the popcorn maker. Past the hot dogs and around two trash cans.

Snow White was on his tail. She was panting just inches away. He felt the slobber on his hind legs.

Mister Whiskers was in big trouble. He kept moving.

Faster . . . faster!

Nine

Arfff! Stacy's cockapoo joined the chase. Behind Mr. Whiskers, two rabbit ears flopped in the air. Dunkum waved his empty dog leash, trying to catch Blinkee.

Meoorsy? Mister Whiskers longed for the cellar at home. So what if it was dark and musty. It was safe!

Just then he heard his girl-person. "Kitty, kitty . . . cookie!" she called.

He glanced behind him. One split second.

Merrrt! No way would he fall for the cookie trick.

A whole trail of things was coming after

him. And he was *purr*ty sure there was no cookie.

Maybe someday he'd have time for a real cookie. If he lived to tell the story!

■ ■ ■

Dee Dee grabbed Carly's hand. "Quick! Help me catch my cat!"

Carly scrambled along after Dee Dee.

They chased the pets through the maze of carnival booths. Two ducks, two dogs, one rabbit, and a crabby cat.

The one and only frog caught the action from a slippery perch. He'd come up for air, next to the principal's dunking chair. The kids were pointing and yelling.

Fran the Ham watched the chase, too. She was safe and dry in Eric's pocket.

Dee Dee and Carly dashed past the ducks. The girls were gaining on Sunday Funnies now.

Then Dee Dee heard it. . . .

Meoowp! Mister Whiskers was crying for help.

She could see him leading the chase. He was headed for the kiddie rides.

Dee Dee sped up. "Hurry, Carly!"

But Carly was out of breath. "I can't run any faster."

Dee Dee lost sight of Mister Whiskers. She stopped running. "We'll never catch him now," she gasped. "Not in all those rides."

The girls peered into the distance. Dee Dee spied Quacker and Jack. They were the last animals into the rides area.

"Come on," Dee Dee said. "We have to get Abby and the others to help us. Our pets could get hurt in there."

Carly followed her back through a tangle of booths and stands.

At last, they found Abby and Stacy. And the other Cul-de-Sac Kids. All of them had been searching in the wrong places.

"The pets are over there," Dee Dee shouted. She pointed toward the busy kiddie rides.

Abby said, "That could be dangerous."

Dee Dee frowned. "What'll we do?"

"Round up all the Cul-de-Sac Kids," she said. "If we stick together, we can catch our pets."

Dee Dee smiled. Abby always talked about sticking together as friends. Maybe that's why she was president of their club.

All nine kids hurried toward the amusement area. There were lots of rides. Even a Ferris wheel.

Dee Dee and Carly passed through the gate for the kiddie rides.

High overhead, the Ferris wheel rose like a tower.

Dee Dee looked up . . . up. Up!

She cupped her hand over her eyes. Then she saw something.

Could it be?

It was!

"Abby, look!" she cried. "My cat's riding on the Ferris wheel!"

The Cul-de-Sac Kids gasped. They stared up at Mister Whiskers.

"He's up there, all right," Jason said. "And I bet he ate my frog!"

Dee Dee was worried. Mister Whiskers *did* look a bit green.

Then someone in the crowd called out, "There's a frog at the dunk tank. He's with the principal."

"Thanks!" Jason said. He ran off to get Croaker.

Dee Dee sighed. Thank goodness! Her cat had behaved himself. He had *not* gobbled down Jason's frog!

Then . . .

Screeeech! There was a horrible, loud scraping sound.

Bam! The Ferris wheel came to a grinding stop.

"Oh no!" shouted Dee Dee. "Look!"

The kids saw where she was pointing. More gulps came from the crowd.

"The Ferris wheel is stuck," Dee Dee hollered. "My cat's on the highest seat!"

And he was. The poor little cat dangled in midair. He stood up and leaned out over the side. He looked down at Dee Dee.

Meoooooooowp!

"We'll help you, kitty!" Dee Dee called to him. "Just don't jump! Please, Mister Whiskers, don't jump!"

But he didn't seem to hear the warning.

Mister Whiskers, eager for freedom, strained his neck. He reached out and pawed the air.

On the ground far below, Dee Dee shook with fear.

Her cul-de-sac friends shouted up to the cat, "Don't jump!"

Dee Dee closed her eyes. She couldn't watch.

She squeezed her eyes tight. "Please, God, don't let Mister Whiskers die."

Ten

Mister Whiskers stared down. Down at the ground.

The hair on his back stuck straight out.

He heard his girl-person calling. She was saying something about having cookies later. Cookies and milk.

Her cheerful voice comforted him. So did the cookie word. Trick or not.

Mister Whiskers pulled his paw back in. He tried to forget about freedom. Bungee jumping without a cord was dumb.

He sat tall. King of kitties.

Then he heard a loud wail.

What was that?

He licked his paws. The paws that had almost nabbed that frog. Almost!

By the way, where *was* Croaker?

From his high perch, Mister Whiskers looked out over the carnival grounds. He could see Croaker's boy-person. Jason, they called him.

Jason was at the dunking tank. So was that bullfrog.

Mister Whiskers felt much too excited. He stretched his neck to see better. He imagined the bullfrog in front of his nose. Right there in the air!

He swung a left power paw. Then jabbed a right. That frog was *hiss*story!

Then . . .

Whoosh!

Mister Whiskers lost his balance.

And . . .

Wheeeee!

He was flying.

No. He was falling.

Down
down . . .
he fell.

■ ■ ■

"Let's catch him!" yelled Dee Dee.

The Cul-de-Sac Kids made their circle. They locked hands.

Ker-plop! Mister Whiskers landed in the middle.

"The Cul-de-Sac Kids stick together," the kids chanted.

Mister Whiskers was a bit dazed by the fall. But he seemed glad for the circle of soft human hands.

Dee Dee hugged him. She covered his head with kisses. "Oh, baby, you're safe," she said.

Just then, the hook-and-ladder truck arrived.

Dee Dee carried her cat over to the fire chief. She explained what happened. "It's a happy ending," she said.

When the fire truck left, Dunkum went looking for the other pets. Stacy, Shawn, Carly, and Jimmy helped, too.

It didn't take long to find Snow White and Sunday Funnies. And Blinkee and the ducks. The merry-go-round stopped. The dizzy pets were rescued.

Dunkum laughed. "Did you ever see a bunch of animals on a kiddie ride?"

Jason jigged around. "They probably thought the horses were for real."

Dee Dee liked the joke.

Mew. Mister Whiskers liked it, too.

The crabby cat caper was over.

Dee Dee's cat lived to *meow* about it. To have cookies and milk at bedtime. And lots of extra kisses and hugs.

■■■

The next day, Dee Dee's father stroked Mister Whiskers. He called him "our pretty kitty."

Dee Dee was glad. Mister Whiskers really *was* part of the family!

He'd learned his lesson. Maybe he'd behave himself from now on. Maybe he wouldn't be such a crab cake.

"Here, kitty, kitty . . . cookie," Dee Dee called. She grinned.

The cookie trick worked.

This time.

About the Author

Beverly Lewis thinks all the Cul-de-Sac Kids are super fun. She clearly remembers growing up on Ruby Street in her Pennsylvania hometown. She and her younger sister, Barbara, played with the same group of friends year after year. Some of those childhood friends appear in her Cul-de-Sac Kids series—disguised, of course! And some of Beverly's own children's friends do, too.

Now Beverly lives with her husband, David, in Colorado, where she enjoys writing books for all ages. She loves to tell stories, but because the Cul-de-Sac Kids series is for children, it will always have a special place in her heart.